D1555127

NOT
TO MENTION
CAMELS

By the same author

Historical Novels

The Fall of Rome
The Flame Is Green
Okla Hannali

Science Fiction Novels

Past Master
Fourth Mansions
Arrive At Easterwine

Fantasy Novels

The Reefs of Earth
Space Chantey
The Devil Is Dead

Short Story Collections

Nine Hundred Grandmothers
Strange Doings
Does Anyone Else Have Something Further To Add?

NOT TO MENTION CAMELS

A Science Fiction Fantasy

R. A. Lafferty

The Bobbs-Merrill Company, Inc.
Indianapolis/New York

Published by the Bobbs-Merrill Company, Inc.
Indianapolis   New York

Designed by Christopher Simon, Simon-Erikson Associates
Manufactured in the United States of America

First printing

Library of Congress Cataloging in Publication Data
Lafferty, R   A
  Not to mention camels.

  I. Title.
PZ4.L1627No [PS3562.A28]   813'.5'4   75-30817
ISBN 0-672-52178-4

There are certain clap-bookers and clap-trappers who are making artificial men, or introducing artificial elements into real men. And these artificial contrivances are then able to stride about on their own movement like godlings.

Tractatus, *Lament of the Times*

NOT
TO MENTION
CAMELS

1

With mortal coil in death uncurled
And body ripe to dump or doff it,
We stand like dummies on a world
Or be like sharpies jumping off it.

"World-Jumper's Ballad"

Pilger Tisman lay in the article of death. He was attended by three outstanding doctors: Funk, Austin, and Ravel; by their numerous aides; by a coroner; and by a brigadier of police. Their care was not to save Pilger's life (there was no chance for that, and no reason for it), but to weigh his death. This business of weighing a death was something new in that place, even though it was said to be common elsewhere. For this weighing, the men used both highly sophisticated and wildly ingenuous equipment.

Pilger Tisman was being executed for his shockingly

1

murderous and irresponsible deeds and behaviors. Public opinion had cried out for his death, and his few supporters were in hiding. He had been sentenced "to die with discomfort." His punishment was quite cruel, but it was not unusual. He was breathing the old ritual gas named Yperite or Mustard, and he had been in absolutely ghastly discomfort before losing consciousness.

"Well, he endured the pain well," Doctor Jude Ravel admitted. "Like a man, as they used to say. Or like a stoic wise-in-death animal. My father used to say that animals had a clear death-accepting ritual; and that if, after accepting the fact of death, the animal should be released from that circumstance, it would go ahead and die anyhow."

"Oh, certainly, certainly," said Doctor Wilcove Funk. "That's known about animals, but Tisman wasn't a wise-in-death animal. He's a frustrated-in-death man. He's a be-trayed-in-death cult figure. A cult figure owes the world a showy death, and Tisman didn't deliver it. He had it planned, I believe, and somehow the pain and the shock jolted it all out of his mind. If that girl had been with him, she could have reminded him of it. She was responsible for many of the showy elements of his career. He went under trying desperately to recall his planned words and gestures, and he's still trying to remember them in his death delirium. If we had equipment just a bit more sophisticated, as we are told that they have in some of the other enclaves, we could still lift those clouded-over words and acts from his flickering mind. As it is, we're denied his heroics. We are cheated."

Another article of Tisman's sentence was that he "should take nothing with him." Most persons, in dying, do not take anything with them. But there are a very few tricky individuals who do. The number of those who took something with them when they died had now risen to one in a hundred of the known cases, and possibly as many of the unknown. With cult figures it was much higher: two out of three at least who took something with them, and who left something behind them that hadn't been there until their going. Cult figures were always tricky. This man Tisman had been tricky in very many ways, and possibly he was tricky in this. It wasn't like him to die blankly.

A difficulty for the death-monitors or death-weighers was that each dying person who took something with him when he went used an individual or peculiar trick to do it. Nothing was standardized. No two persons, apparently, had ever used the same device. The tracing technique was quite new in this place, but already the catalogue of tricks numbered more than a hundred. This made the carrying-forward of material or weighable substance difficult to prevent.

The thing that most dying persons took forward with them—this was no more than an instrumental guess—was probably memory. Or it was identity. Or it was consciousness (or the capacity for consciousness, for it was mostly unconscious persons who made the leap). Were these three things the same? At least all of them were weighable.

Did one who took something forward with him always leave something extra behind also? Probably. It couldn't always be detected immediately—perhaps it wasn't always weighable; but the departing ones who took something with them did seem always to leave a new and compensating thing in its place. Cult figures particularly did often leave a fast-spreading residue (can a newly appearing thing be called a residue?) in place of what they took with them. The thing taken and the thing left may have been two halves of a unity, and it threatened to crush a world like a shell between the riven halves. The world was hard shelled, though, and very seldom was it actually crushed by such a circumstance.

In earlier times, those who carried such minimum personal baggage (memory, identity, consciousness) forward with them from the death drama did often have after-appearances that were nothing worse than harmless ghosts. But in these recent decades, and as the cults had evolved into a new natural force, the tricky departing ones seemed able to erect horrendous ghost worlds or counterworlds that impinged, sometimes physically, upon the real world. The encounters with these intrusive worlds were dislocating, disturbing, eroding, and fright-inducing in their effects. And they were *not* harmless.

"As a hulk I don't like him," Doctor Jon Austin said. "I don't really see how anyone could like him as a hulk, or as a man, as well as I had known him. But cult figures are loved. They have devoted followings. They have magnetic effects. Do you understand how this Tisman could have been loved by anyone?"

"I half understand it," said Doctor Wilcove Funk.

"It may be that I understand the other half of it," said Doctor Jude Ravel. "We two would never understand the same half of anything."

"We have paralyzed all his centers," Doctor Wilcove Funk said to the room at large, "even some of the involved centers whose purpose we do not understand. We have muted but not quite silenced his call-tone or person-tone. We have dimmed his corona spectrum, but we sure have not been able to put it out. That is really all we can do. The next move is up to him.

"It would seem that his numbed areas could not translate their data to any point beyond. And yet we know of cases where absolutely dead areas have done so. We will see. We've been tricked before, and by persons of lesser reputation than this man. We learn, with every person who slips by us, to guard a little better against this sort of encounter. We still don't know what death is, but we do know that nothing ever winds all the way down without winding something else up."

Doctor Funk was a man with a huge head, with heavy orbital ridges; with a protruding muzzle on him that made a true chin unnecessary and impossible; with a large back-brain; and with a great good humor. He was a tremendous man with a steep amount of animal in him, and with a sharp apperception of things in between.

But the dying Pilger Tisman had an even larger back-brain. How was there room for it? It was almost a case of the inside of his skull being bigger than the outside. And as to the humor of Tisman—well, those who had known him extensively had testified that he had a large, craggy, towering humor, outrageous, noisy, overflowing, and fearsome. But it was not always a good humor. Those assisting at his death were all secretly afraid that he would give them a stroke of his strong humor even out of his death delirium.

"It is inconsiderate for any man to take so long a time to die," the brigadier of police said testily. "Are you sure we're more likely to muff it if we hurry it along? Or have some of you the compassionate sickness?"

"Yes, I have the compassionate sickness," Doctor Funk said. "And we're not sure which way we're most likely to muff it. We're keeping records, as you know, and we will try to determine that as we determine other things."

Doctor Funk regarded the dying Tisman with sympathy and kindred feeling, even though he agreed that Tisman was unnecessarily slow about giving up the ghost. Funk's giant hands were compassionate as he monitored the guttering brain and body of Tisman. It was the centralized memory prints that he worried about, that area of abridgments and handy essences that nearly duplicated, in highly compressed form, the gangling memory that ran all through the brain itself. This was the *cerebral juglans,* that small nodule whose purpose and content had but lately been discovered. Funk marred the *juglans,* the "remembering acorn," but what would be the effect of his marring it? The *juglans* was a fat composite of chemical fixes and electrical charges that inhabited the patterned wrinkles and grooves of that small nodule; and it was the containing nodule itself, that which seemed always on the nervous edge of explosion. But it was the patterns, even the empty patterns, that held the power. Content and detail were not important on this level. Patterns could always create their own new detail. Taking the patterns away might seem like stealing holes or tunnels: not to be done. But it was often done nowadays.

"There was never such a call-tone or person-tone as this man has," Doctor Jude Ravel said admiringly. "It hardly needs amplifying. I believe that a person of exceptionally acute hearing would be able to pick it up with his bare ears. It is too rough and rambunctious to be a musical tone, and yet it has almost infinite depth and texture to it. It is a whole orchestra full of randy harmonics, and a mighty randy orchestra it is. In some cases, the person-tone or the call-tone will make a very good résumé of a man. Not here. Tisman can't be expressed by one sense, but this tone is a sort of signature of this man. No other person, thank the god of ears, could ever sound that sound."

Doctor Ravel was talking about Tisman's call-tone, a nonchromatic aspect of the body corona translated into audio and then greatly amplified.

"And yet, remarkable man that Tisman was, incandescent cult figure that he was, he leaves behind him only one powerful friend and one powerful enemy," Doctor Jon Austin said. "And of his cult, it is believed that only two members remain faithful to him. If so, where are they?"

"I want to hear that tone of the man Tisman extinguished," the brigadier of police said solidly. "I want to hear it extinguished at exactly the same time that I see the man himself extinguished, that I see his life go out. I hate these after-sounds from a dead man. They mean that an execution has been bungled, and I'll not accept a bungle in this one. Do not fool with the amplification! And do not try to fool me. I want *all* of him to expire, evenly, quickly, and forever. I do not want an echo, or any afterglow or after-sound."

It had been said that this brigadier of police was firmly under the finger of the one powerful enemy of Tisman. But the brigadier seemed to be finding the hatred of Tisman in his own person.

"If the man is able to evade our nets and to leap forward, the tone of the man will also make the jump—last of all," Doctor Ravel said. "It's the sign that a man has been extinguished, or has escaped being extinguished. If he does leap forward, the tone will be heard again, an instant after the body's death. If the man has succeeded, the tone will be heard triumphant, and from a location outside of the body. And it will not need amplification. And sometimes that tone will seem to mock."

"That man-tone had better *not* be heard from some location outside the body," the brigadier of police stated with that menace of voice that all brigadiers of police develop. "I said that I wanted to hear that tone extinguished at the same time that I see that man and his life extinguished. It had better not sound again. And it had better not mock."

"Here is something new in light," Doctor Jon Austin said with pleasant interest, "and something new in color. Though each person's aura is unique, some are crankily more unique than others; and Tisman's is uniqueness itself. Since we first learned to translate the electrical shell that is called aura into light and color, there hasn't been a personal spectrum like this. There must be a hundred nonchromatic colors in it. Ah, those grays, those silvers, those brasses, that pulsating pallidness! And some of those shinings and shimmers are cut loose from any color at all. Even the blackness writhes and shines. There are areas of light that cannot be fractured at all, that will not break down into any components. I tell you that this man is a dazzle!

"Of course, pyrotechnics themselves are easy. It is almost to take cheap advantage of the world to use them at all. But pyrotechnic flesh is a little different case; it is the case of Pilger Tisman and of many of the cult figures. I wonder if pyrotechnic flesh is all that is really required of a cult figure. There may be a bit more than that to be found in this man."

"Why doesn't he die?" the brigadier of police asked with a peevishness that was almost a pout. "His lungs have to be entirely burned up. His brain is cooked. His heart ruptured three minutes ago. A few aspects of him have already tried to climb over the wall to get out, and we've knocked each of them back into the flame. Don't let anything climb over the wall when it comes to the end! I want Tisman dead! I want him all dead at the same time, with no pieces hanging over the edges of him. And that time is now."

"It never happens that way, Salvatore," the coroner told the brigadier. "Dying is always a series of reactions and backlashes. Nobody ever died all at once. Ah, there's his last throe, I'll wager. He can't regain consciousness, of course, but there's a stirring and coherence in the cellar of his mind, though it's in the occipital region of his brain. His brain is now emitting impulses in the delta pattern (this isn't common for one who is unconscious, and it certainly isn't common for a world-jumper; it's a trick, a personal trick): a pattern of about three counts a second. Tisman is sending, he's probing, he's getting ready for a leap. He's gauging the footholds and handholds on the other side before he makes the grand jump out over the chasm."

"Stomp on his damned fingers!" the brigadier of police crackled. "Don't give him a handhold. Don't give him any hold at all. We want him dead and done for."

"He's dead," Doctor Wilcove Funk said tightly. "We can't know yet, maybe ever, whether he succeeded in his leap or not. The canniest of jumpers sometimes do not leap straight across. Some of them leap upstream for the cliff-faces there.

Some of them jump for the downstream bluffs. Some of them wade through shoal water, and some of them climb immeasurable heights in their attempt to get across and away. There were never such mountain-climbers or abyss-leapers as these outlaw world-jumpers in the moments of their gateway deaths."

"You seem to know a lot about the topology of the other side," Doctor Ravel chided.

"The topology of the other *sides*," Doctor Funk said. "They are legion."

Pilger Tisman was dead. His heart and breath and heat were gone. His voltage was gone. The tumultuous vinegar of his chemistry was dried and dead. His brain waves were in what has humorously been called the omega pattern—zero per second. His tone was extinguished. His colorful aura went out. His memory center, the abridgments and essences that filled up that small *cerebral juglans,* was still fat and full, fossilized and frozen—and unescaped. Tisman was dead. This was an "end of pyrotechnics."

For about three seconds.

Then that centralized memory deposit collapsed as its fat content was removed in electrical charge and chemical fix and pattern. This was an absolute physical theft from the body, one that could be clearly recorded. Someone had stolen the meat from that acorn.

The aura dazzled and shimmered again, but not in the neighborhood of the body. It was at some distance in that medical amphitheater, and then it flicked out through the walls, out of the region, out of the world. The person-tone of the dead man sounded again, clear, without any translation or amplification, and it also was located outside of the vessel of the body. The tone sounded triumphant in its resurrection, and it did mock with a biting mockery. Then it was gone; not gone out, but gone away from there in a swoop.

"I told you that I wanted him dead and done for!" the

brigadier shouted in white anger. "You've bungled it, the bunch of you! You can't even kill a man definitively. Heads will roll, I tell you!" And the brigadier stomped out.

Doctor Ravel, with a grimace, whistled a couple of bars of that current song hit, "Heads Will Roll." But the humor of it deepened and lowered when the person-tone of dead Tisman took up the same haunting tune. There was a bit of horror gnawing at them in the area there, but also some ultra-purple fun.

"I said that I half understood how he might have been loved," Doctor Funk said. "Now I understand it a bit more than half. But what have we here? Ah, ulp, nothing."

Well, Tisman had taken something with him: his memory, his identity, and the container for his consciousness. These are things that can be weighed, and they were. But had Tisman left any new and compensating thing in the place of what he had taken? Likely he had. And likely it was stolen, to be suppressed, by the first of the monitors who discovered it.

Doctor Wilcove Funk, taken by strange impulse, concealed the thing and held it in his hand. He hid it pretty well there, and he hid fairly well the fact that the thing shone through the flesh and bones of his hand. And he concealed, for a few days, the fact that it overflowed his hand and occupied the world, in a very thin but complete manner. Well, the world at any one time is pretty completely occupied by some several dozens of such very thin things, very diluted things. They aren't much noticed, but anyone who is occupied in the careful weighing of the world would be able to weigh these all-extending thin things also.

"It always puzzles me what happens to the data," the pale Doctor Ravel mused. He always paled a bit when a jump death was successful. Such things always drew energy from every sensitive person present. "It's as though one went back to play again an old record or tape or cassette and found that all the sound-fossils had been erased or scraped clean. But how does one erase a brain? What could have happened to those particular signature brain tracks of Tisman? He could at least have left us the footprints of where they had been, couldn't he? Or are the footprints the essence of it all? It may be that valid footprints can create a new person to fill them."

"Yeah, he took them with him," Doctor Funk said, disappointed that they had failed to catch these things in their careful nets, defeated once more in this project, but a trifle glad that this prey had escaped their hunting. "He took a lot of things with him, many more than most jumpers take. And if he left a token, well, he left it to be hidden. This man Tisman was an adept."

"At what?" Doctor Austin asked.

"At dying, of course. He may even remember doing it," Funk said. "Well, he escaped our nets. He got away. He world-jumped."

"Where to?" Doctor Ravel asked him sharply.

"I don't know," Funk answered with a touch of sorrow. "There are shadow worlds all around us when we deal with such obstreperous dying folks. I can't touch the worlds myself, or see them. I seem to get a small noise from them sometimes, though, a noise that is in my own tone. We try to net knowledge here, of course, but I'm not too sorry when a dead man escapes us with something much thinner than his skin. I can't see what law is broken by a dead man jumping to another milieu. When they fight extinction hard enough, I find that I'm partisan to their fight. It is very hard to enforce laws against dead men in any case."

"I always feel guilty when I write 'dead' to the record of one of these jumping persons," the short-spoken coroner told them. "There should be several special categories for them: possibly, 'Dead, subject to continuance,' or, 'Not so dead as all that.' Alive and dead surely aren't the only two alternatives."

But, "Adept at dying" or not, "Not so dead as all that" or not, Pilger Tisman was buried later that day.

There seemed to be only one mourner, Maria del Mar, a young and taut-faced girl about whom little is known other than that she was a cult follower of the cult figure Tisman.

Wait! There was another, but he hung back at some distance. He mourned with a silent, sobbing motion, but he did not come near to the burying. He was named Jacob del Mar; he was a brother of Maria, and he was another cult follower of Tisman.

The powerful friend and the powerful enemy of Tisman were not in evidence.

All of this happened about fifteen years before our subsequent action. Or it may be that a fifteen-year leap to upstream cliffs had created the illusion of such an interval. There is no proved correlation between the different worlds.

2

With stones for bread, for fishes snakes,
For men synthetic leaders chilly,
The god Electronus now makes
Creations of Old God look silly.

Neo-Creational Procedures File

It was once believed, by many speculative scientists, that there might be dozens of billions of life-supporting worlds in the universes. These worlds were thought to be scattered throughout space in whatever were the more apt or green or fortunate spots for growing worlds. This multiplicity of worlds was assumed even before the discovery of a Prime World from which the multiplicity might proceed. It was not even understood then that there must be a prime before there can be a procession. Nevertheless, these speculative scientists were correct.

And it was once believed, by many nonscientists and pseudoscientists and fringe people, that there might be—in quite a different way from the first instance—dozens of billions of life-supporting worlds in the universes. But the fringies and nonsuches and pseudos understood this numeration of worlds to be of a slightly different arrangement and order than the hardhead scientists had supposed. These worlds were not to be scattered throughout space. There was not any space in such scatterable sense. These worlds were all to occupy the same familiar local space. They were the tree-worlds or the branch-worlds or the crossroad-worlds, and there was only one tree that they might grow upon. The nons and pseudos and fringies sometimes called them the alternate worlds. And the persons of these wide-eyed groups were quite correct in their suppositions.

There was a third belief that was held by many determined and brilliant, though spotty, folks. This was the belief that there was only one world and that all possible persons were in it. This belief maintained that there were not even dozens of billions of souls or persons in that one world; that, in fact, there were only about three and a half billion souls available; and that there could be no more ever. And it maintained that almost all of the possible souls were already bodied in the world at this present time; that a firm limit would soon make itself felt; or that there would be catastrophe. There were others, of the same sort but of slightly different views, who said that all souls had been poured into flesh long ago, and that three of every four persons in the world now were not true persons but only reflections of persons. This belief was that the prime count was for prime souls only, and that all others were shadow souls or derivative persons who did not have a like force, who were not real at all in a strict sense. These several grouped beliefs were mainly about the transmigration of souls, the jumping from death to life in another body, sometimes remembering what had gone before, more often forgetting. And the persons who held these several similar beliefs were absolutely right to hold them.

And at the same time that these three true theories were current, it was maintained by at least one person (his name was Pilgrim Dusmano) that there was no contradiction in these theories and no reason for conflict: that these three beliefs were only three aspects of the same thing, if, that is, one should take a tri-mental view of space and of being and of several other things.

The space of the countless universes—this was Pilgrim's contention—was identical with the familiar local space and was in no way larger than that local space. One space did not contain the other; one space did not go beyond the other; they were of the same measure. A man with a good right arm might throw a stone clear across space, but of course it would be an endless rock that he threw.

"My presumption," Pilgrim Dusmano was saying to his students, "—for I cannot call it theory, since, once it is entertained at all, it goes beyond itself and makes all theories obsolete—my arrogant presumption and absolute claim is that there are these dozens of billions of alternate worlds right here right now. My claim requires a new way of looking at space and a new way of looking at being. Since these new ways are required, they will be supplied. The multiple worlds in the space that the scientists have loved for so long are really out there. Ah, but 'Out There' is also 'In Here.' The apparent celestial locations of distant galaxies are but notes upon the sky maps for the purpose of giving the names of those clusters in cipher, for there is no room to write them down all in one place; the notes must be written in the margins. This requires a new way of looking at margins, which are spaces outside of accepted spaces. The distant locations are true ones, however. But here we run into the problem of bi-location. For, wherever else all the worlds are, they are also all in one place—here."

"I don't understand old Dusmano at all in this world," said James Morey, a pleasant young man who was a student of Pilgrim Dusmano. "Well, then, since I do not understand him at all in this world, and if his presumptions have any validity at all, it must be that some alternate me in some alternate world understands him. There have been alternate selves of me who really revered him, and I don't know why that should have been so. It may be that his effect is cumulative. But, as of now, he doesn't seem like much."

"Amorality is implicit as a total thing in my claim," Dusmano was saying, "or it is implicit in all cases except one out of dozens of billions. Recompense cannot be real; debt and guilt are not real; punishment and death are only illusions. We do not die. We pass into an alternate world and we live again there. This has been going on for as long as mankind and its bodies and souls have been going on. But perhaps we are now able to improve this metacosmosis, this transmigration of worlds. Our world-jumping need not be random. It should be the object of our careful study.

"Some of you here may be enamored of your own childhoods. Well, then, repeat your childhoods, and do it as often as you wish. And do it in as many different costumes as you wish. It may be well for you to die, in the common understanding of that word, in childhood to get back to that time more easily. The eldest of you here is not more than twenty years old; you are still children. If you want to be of an earlier age, you have only to leap upstream in your next world-jumping. Or do you like it as it is now? Leave it as it is, then. Do not jump unnecessarily. Go on for another year, or two, or three. Then kill yourselves by the method of your own choice. It isn't final. And you can remember that it is *you* who jump. You can even remember much of your present life, in hooded form perhaps, if—well, you can remember it if you *remember* to remember. There are certain distractions in every death, and you must learn to ignore some of them. The continuity of memories requires a certain attention at the moment of dying. You can, within reason, select the quality of life you wish to jump to. And you can, with a little practice, return at almost any age you wish. And there's nice choice and wide variety if you bring a stubborn mentality to bear on the selection. There are, for instance, enclaves where boy children are born with beards and moustaches, and where females are born figured and busted and in full speech. Those are only examples, but they are true ones.

"Myself, I like the young adult role. I came here fifteen year ago, to age fifteen. I'll go on with it now for another ten years. Then I'll shift again. Ah, I recall one environs where the young male adults were horned and hoofed during the rutting season. Oh, that season! For a six-week interlude, there is nothing like it. I sometimes believe that I will go back there every springtime. It's one of the most easily attained of all the environs.

"Is it real? you ask. Oh, not completely real. I'd say that it's about as real as the world we're in now."

"I don't understand Mr. Dusmano either," Howard Praise mumbled. "He's a little unreal when he implies that the worlds are a little unreal. I'm on the edge of joining his cult, but what if there is nothing in him at all?"

Then Howard spoke aloud. "Sir, are you really suggesting that we kill ourselves?"

"Suggesting it, yes," Dusmano said pleasantly, "but it isn't a weighted suggestion. It's better to have your dying under your own control than under the misdirection of others. After all, death is seldom final. It is so only in one very rare case. It is one of the things that one would best do for himself. Self-destruction is one strong possibility that is always open to us. We should use this flexibility of the universes. It's harder, though, when we die at the last minute. We sacrifice very much flexibility when we do that, and our reappearances will be duller instead of brighter. There are too many persons who go always from dull to still duller lives, and there may be no cure for them. They do not remember, they do not scheme, they do not seize. But I bring words to you bright young people here today: *Everything is allowed to you.* And I cannot see any limit to the number or spaciousness of the lives you will be able to live."

"Mr. Dusmano is right, of course, but I don't understand him," said Rhinestone Suderman, a large, fair-haired young female person. "I keep saying there's no way I could ever be attracted to him. And I keep knowing I'm wrong every time I say it."

"Mr. Dusmano is wrong, of course, and I *do* understand him," said Mary Morey, a freckled, rusty-haired, unlarge girl who was in the middle of a tangled and worried adolescence. It would be wrong to say that Mary was bug-eyed, although both her eyes were in quite high relief. "But I am a partisan of his. I am with him all the way, to the grave and beyond, to an endless series of graves and a tedious series of beyonds. And he really isn't very much: hardly anything at all. Why am I caught up by a daemon like him?"

And then Mary said in a louder voice, "What is the catch to it, Mr. Dusmano? I've asked you before, often, in other places, at other times. I forget where or when they were, since I've only known you for this week here. But there is always a catch. What is the catch that weighs on the other side of the balance?"

"It weighs so lightly that we will not even mention it," Pilgrim Dusmano assured Mary and the class. "There are billions of chances against its ever happening to you. So we will disregard the slim chance that the evil might fall."

"But there *is* one chance that it will all go wrong?" Mary asked. "Anything that can be named has its chance of happening. And we know that rational odds do not prevail in random anachronicities."

"How do we know that?" Pilgrim asked.

"It says that in our arithmetic book," Mary answered. "But the one bad case, if it comes, might be billions of times more severe than all the good cases, out of compensation. There *is* a catch. Name the catch to us."

"No! I'll not name it to you! I'll not think of it at all!" Pilgrim Dusmano said with sudden starkness. "I'll limn out the bright opportunities for you this morning, and that is all there will be time for. That is all there is ever going to be time for. Never, never think of the extremely improbable failure. That way is madness."

In due time, Pilgrim Dusmano completed his lecture to the young people; then he left them. And they were about to leave.

"Wait a bit," Rhinestone Suderman told them all. "Is anyone here interested in forming a Pilgrim Dusmano cult?"

"But he's so mixed up," Howard Praise muttered.

"Say that he's 'chaotic,' rather," Rhinestone suggested. "This gives us more scope. In one of the mythologies, great things were brought out of chaos. And if we must start a cult, let us start it on the broadest possible basis: chaos. Dusmano is our man, the chaotic man, soon to be more than man, with our aid."

"But *must* we start a cult?" James Morey asked with a little resentment.

"Of course we must. We're compelled to," Rhinestone said.

"Compelled to? By what?" Howard Praise wanted to know.

"By a compulsion, of course. By a blind compulsion. All cults are started by such compulsions."

But, later that morning, Pilgrim did give a name to that narrow foul chance that lurked so impossibly small in the statistics.

"The name of the obdurate thing is Prime World," he told his associate and one powerful friend, Noah Zontik. "Its prospects are as small as a grain of sand compared to a solar system medium in size. That's about what the contrary chance amounts to."

"A grain of sand is a nuisance even in a giant's shoe," Noah said. "Well, *is* there really such a thing as Prime World?"

"I think so. In simple mathematics, there has to be one, or there has *to have been* a Prime World. It would have been best to posit Prime World first of all, to derive from it and to multiply the derivations, and then to destroy the prime original, which was sure to have been inferior. But the Lord of the Worlds doesn't always seem to know what best to do with his own devices, and in simple ethics there has to be a Prime World now. Some first object has to have cast the first shadow; and that shadow-caster must remain for proof, and to teach humility to the universe. But Prime World has surely long since been—pardon me, Noah—overshadowed by its shadows."

They were talking in the Prismatic Room of the Personage Club.

"Why is even the possibility of a Prime World so much of a threat to you, Pilgrim?"

"Because logic would prevail on Prime World. That is so on the word of leaders in a dozen sciences and speculations. And there is nothing so irrational as logic. It has all the narrow sequence of an old mule track. It is one-dimensional and one-directional. It would be murderous to such a man as myself, eternally murderous. *They keep accounts* on Prime World; ultimate accounts, I mean. They keep crabbed, careful, fetishistic accounts. Oh, Noah, would I ever have to pay!"

"But if it were not for the possibility of being trapped there, would you not like to see Prime World sometime, if only for its absolute uniqueness?"

"Never, Noah, never. It could be called unique only in its being the dullest of all possible worlds. Prime World is where all the sordidness of mythology is still in existence. It is where compensation is calculated and extracted. It is the world where all facts are hard and there is no buoyancy at all. It is the base and anchor of the four final or eschatological things. Thankfully, there are no final things attached to any of the other worlds. Prime is the fetish world where there must be a solid reality corresponding to every speculation, where the very metaphors are material and weighted objects. It is the world of muck and of bottomless sloughs for a bottoming-earth, and of a sky coming down far too low for a ceiling. I mean thoroughly material mud, and detailed, textured sky. It's the world of sinewy hands gripping one with no release; it's the place of delirious minds that permit no deviation. The absolute logic of total delirium is the most fearful thing to be found anywhere. Prime World is murk, it is mud, it is miasmic fever. It would not be possible to world-jump from Prime. Hairy and fetish hands coming out of that earth would grip one about the ankles, and grip with bone-crushing strength. According to students of that dark contingency, there are only two ways off of Prime World. And the one of the two that sounds the most bearable to me is named hell."

"Pilgrim, does your theory, or your presumption—or claim, as you call it—have room for prime people and for derivative people?"

Pilgrim twisted a small scarf in his almost womanly hands. "This is the scarf with which I do small miracles," he said, "miracles with an eye to my cult. But first, Noah, do not parallel prime world with prime people. There is mere verbal coincidence there."

"First, Pilgrim, there can never be mere verbal coincidence.

Every coincidence goes beyond itself. There are no accidents; these are your own words somewhere."

"My own words in another context. All right, Noah; yes, my presumption has room, barely room, for prime people. We are open on that subject. There do seem to be multitudes of derivative people and only a few of us primes."

"Then you consider yourself to be a prime person, Pilgrim?"

"Certainly, Noah, if there are such. How could I not be prime?"

"But suppose that there *is* an analogy between prime people and Prime World. And, Pilgrim, there is. What if the prime people, like Prime World, are all sordid and crabbed and careful and fetishistic? What if they are logical and dull? What if they are narrow—"

"No, no!"

"Yes, Pilgrim, yes. What if the prime people are murky and mucky and miasmic? What if the prime people are those with the sinewy, gripping hands and the delirious minds? In the beginning there were sinew and delirium. Where would that leave you?"

"Noah, you are making an upside-down, soaring joke, like an eagle joking in the sky. I've seen them, very early in the mornings, roll over like that on the wing. And this scares the world. The world believes, for a moment, that it has disappeared when the eagle can no longer see it, when the eagle looks down and sees only sky. The world does not think clearly in the early mornings. No, Noah, the world hasn't ended. You've just made an eagle fly upside-down for an instant. Do not shake me with such ideas! Do not turn me upside-down! If the prime people were the degraded ones, it would leave me with no place at all to stand."

"Yes, Pilgrim, it leaves you with everywhere to stand and to saunter. For you do stand, and you do stride on the successive, or alternate, worlds as your stepping stones. You will not be hemmed in by anything, so why will you be hemmed in by two words? The fact is that you are *not* any prime person at all. You are a derivative."

"Noah, whatever else I am, I am an authentic original. I could never be a derivative." Pilgrim twisted his scarf, that with which he worked small miracles, with a certain petulance.

"No!" Noah said sharply. "You are not a dull, muddy, logical, fevered, low-sky original, Pilgrim. You are an exciting, though shallow, derivative. Really, you are entirely too extravagant and flamboyant to be in any way a prime person. I believe that you had your origin in the compensating imagination of some particularly dull individual, some prime person indeed. You are a projection, even a secondary projection, and you catch the light, as do all such gaseous projections. Dull flesh cannot catch the light like that, Pilgrim. It cannot become such a dazzle, such a shimmering sundog. Only ionized gas can shine with such light. And the most shining gas of all is swamp gas, always charged and luminescent, and always the projection of the most dismal swamp."

"Stop it, Noah, stop it," Pilgrim moaned.

"Let me tell you a little bit more about the Prime World of prime people, Pilgrim. It is the uninfused world, the grubby world, the spiritualist world, the quack world, the Fortean world. That world is real, and all others are shadows of it. You say this, but you are afraid to mean it, and you are afraid to acknowledge yourself a citizen of it. But your only alternative is to own yourself to be a reflected and not a real person. On Prime World, fish and rocks and blood do indeed fall on the earth out of low and stationary skies. For these are stale skies and do not turn. One can reach those skies with stones thrown by a ballista, and such shots will bring other stones falling in showers onto prime earth. Everything moves very slowly on prime, like objects moved by poltergeists. It is like things moving underwater. It is things moving in prime atmosphere and the reek and heaviness of it. There are vulgar shouts out of that lowering sky. Why not? There are giants living up there, dimwit giants who are the pride of prime. This is the original world, and the dimwits are the original people. What, Pilgrim—would you swallow only half a camel? And what will you do with the rest of it?"

"You joke, Noah," Pilgrim cried with a nervous heartiness. "And this isn't an upside-down eagle joke; it's a malodorous rock-shrew joke. How those foul things can attack the quick flesh of one! But I must go now. At once."

The scarf that Pilgrim had been twisting in his hands now overflowed or exploded into a mantle or a cloak. Arrayed in this, Pilgrim went right through the walls of the Prismatic Room and the Personage Club in incipient flight. Noah Zontik stepped to a window and watched Pilgrim ascend the incandescent blue air of the outdoors in slanting, soaring flight. He had a finesse beyond that of any bird. A bird doesn't understand how to pose in the air, how to get the most from his natural lines, how to live a lyric in quick stanzas of flight. Pilgrim covered half a city in the ticking off of a dozen seconds. It was perfection.

"I never will know how he does such things," Noah Zontik muttered in hoarse wonder. "But, really, it's a scruffy little handful of tricks and miracles that he has. Are they enough to make him into an authentic cult figure?"

Pilgrim Dusmano, halfway across town, descended from his flight into the interior of an unspecified house. He quickly killed a startled man there.

"A bit casual, was it not?" the victim rasped with his dying breath.

Well, yes, it was too casual. It was badly done, without style, without timing, without elegance, without taste, completely without drama. It was a sordid and common thing, not something out of the soaring freedom. It was a prime world sort of gaffe. But was it a prime person sort of clumsiness, or a derivative kind of gaucherie?

"This will have to be heavily redacted, revised, scripted, dramatized, before it can enter into the gestes of my cult," Pilgrim thought, but he was uncertain in his feelings. The killing was something that had to be done for expediency, but doing it badly was not in any way expedient. And Pilgrim didn't know where he had gone wrong in his presentation.

"It's no good saying that nobody saw the maladroit thing except myself. Such busts are written plainly on the air itself for everyone to read. I'll get it revised as much as I can."

Pilgrim soared through walls again to an unobtrusive street. He stood on his feet there. "Enough of small miracles for one morning," he thought. He twisted the flowing mantle-cloak back into a small scarf. He sauntered along the way and flew no more for that while.

"I am diminished," said the one powerful enemy of Pilgrim Dusmano in that environs. The enemy wrestled with his dark intuition in his murky headquarters. "I have just been slain in one of my limbs," he said, "and it was done without drama. Oh God, completely without drama! A hog would deserve more drama than that in having his throat cut. It is the creature named Dusmano who has done it. I don't call him a man; I don't know what he is. I believe he is a giant insect in the form of a man, one veined with green scum and inelegant instincts. Ah, I'd like to know what color blood that fellow bleeds."

This one powerful enemy of Pilgrim Dusmano was named Cyrus Evenhand, and he was accounted a good man. He was a serious, pleasant, slow-thinking but sure-thinking man of rough appearance. His eight henchmen (seven now, for Pilgrim had just killed one) were much swifter of thought, much more suave, much more urbane than was Evenhand.

They were all men of public position, for which reason their names will not be given here. Cognomens, yes; but not their names.

Evenhand himself worked behind a mask, and the public didn't guess the connection between his two main identities. He was behind the scenes always, a big, gently awkward man with stumbling insights and clumsy power.

"It's easy enough to kill this Pilgrim Dusmano," one of the henchmen suggested. "It can be done in a quick moment and forgotten about before noon. The problem isn't that tall, Evenhand. You make mountains out of middens."

"How else are mountains ever made? Even if we sentence him by kangaroo, it must be a fair trial and a fair sentence. But this Dusmano has been killed before, or parallels of him have been. These are fuzzy things on removed planes, and we can't have direct knowledge of them. But the killings weren't final. When you fumble the killing of a man, he loses respect for you. That his more immediate killing should be a final one will depend, I believe, on the shape of the way we kill him."

"When you finish with the riddles, then you may be able to tell us what you have in mind," another of the henchmen said, "and we may be able to help you." These men all had very great respect for Evenhand, but sometimes he seemed unnecessarily slow in his actions and irritatingly pure in his motives.

Only three of the henchmen were present physically. Two others were present by voice-and-vision device, and two by voice hookup only. And the one who had just been killed was present by psychic vehicle; but the rules would not allow him to speak at this time.

"Well, thank you, gentlemen," Evenhand was saying lamely. "We don't have to act today, but we will act before the season has turned over. You all be thinking about it."

"Thinking about what?" another of the henchmen asked

with exasperation. "You haven't given us any clear idea of what you have in mind. 'The shape of the way we kill him' be damned! You can count on us, Evenhand, but first you have to learn to count."

"Well, Evenhand, about this Pilgrim. *Do* you want to know what color blood he bleeds?" a fourth henchman asked.

"Yes," said big unpolished Evenhand. "I want to know that."

"I'll find out," the henchman said.

Pilgrim Dusmano had gone to war with a powerful and secret apparatus, and he had drawn first death in that war.

"I don't know what he's done now, but he's just made another of his lightning strikes," Noah Zontik had told himself, a bit after he had seen Pilgrim soar off into the steep air that morning. "I felt it, and I shivered. This Dusmano is the trickiest friend or client any man ever had. He's the big millstone around my neck. He's the punishment from God."

God had once told Noah Zontik, told it to his battered inner ear, "Every man needs one powerful friend who will be surety for him. This man who is sometimes named Pilgrim will need you for his friend and shield. No one else will serve for this job at all, for he's a difficult one. Now you will be responsible for him. I cannot find anyone else capable of handling the job, and I've considered a great number. You will be responsible for him in every way. If he goes to hell for a final place, you will go there too."

"And who will be responsible for me?" Noah Zontik asked God as reasonably as he could.

God told Noah a name. Noah barely recognized it. "That man will be responsible for me?" Noah asked.

"Yes. Don't make his job too hard for him."

This was an unreal business. The man didn't mean much to Noah. Then Noah forgot both the man and his name. What to do?

"I forgot the name and the man you told me," Noah said fearfully. "Tell me again."

God told him again. It still seemed unreal. Noah forgot the name and man again. And he was ashamed to ask once more for the information. It was a nervous situation.

"It is hard to hold an umbrella over so protean a man as Pilgrim Dusmano," Noah continued to himself on that latter day. "And if it's hard for me, it would be impossible for anyone else. I'll do my best."

Noah Zontik was sometimes known as the Umbrella. He dealt in shielding, in protection, in hiding persons both guilty and innocent, in thwarting prosecutors and trackers. He was good luck against the inundations and torrents such as may sweep over a person. He was a good man and a crafty man, but he had dirty hands always from the sort of business he was engaged in. He was a professional.

But he would never have taken Pilgrim on as a client except on a direct order from God. There was something familiar about it from the first, as though he had been through that before. And Noah would never have come to love Pilgrim in any natural order of things. Noah suspected that he had done this also on a direct order from someone, but not from God. Pilgrim was unlovable, and now he was becoming a cult figure. The young people of his cult, those who really loved him, were all ashamed of the fact. With them it was a dirty and secret vice. And Noah hadn't the excuse of being a young person. It was an unpleasant sort of happiness that attached to the Dusmano cult, and particularly to those who were on the fringes of the cult.

3

Nineveh, in which there are more than a hundred and twenty thousand persons that know not how to distinguish their right hand from their left, not to mention many camels.

God

Even in a single world, Pilgrim Dusmano lived half a dozen simultaneous lives. Every morning he attended to the seedbed or seminary of selected students at Rampart University. No matter what he did, if he followed any sort of deep plan, he would always need small and select groups of outstanding people, generation after generation of them. And the best way to get them was to grow them in such seedbeds as this. Pilgrim did not literally plant and grow these young people, but he did shape them to his own liking.

29

And he did graft certain little brain scions of his own selection onto all of them.

It would seem that a jumper like Pilgrim would not be around in one environs long enough to have a need for generation after generation of select groups. But to think this way is to disregard Dunlunk's Fifth Law: "Any action in any world will inevitably set up parallel actions in parallel worlds." So the shaping of the plastic younglings on this orb would shape their correspondence-integers on corresponding orbs. It would shape them less and still less according to distance in attitude and space and time, but it would always shape them somewhat.

There's a proverb about casting bread on waters and its coming back to one a hundredfold. Well, it won't come back a hundredfold to everyone; there are many persons who will get back no bread at all. But one who is in on this exchange early and carefully can always depend on an increase of bread. Pilgrim was always well organized as to his corresponding persons. The different integers of him helped one another, for they were all the same person on the final plane. And this cultivating of the young grain, with bread-casting in mind, was to provide for multiple eventualities. It is always a queasy feeling to go into a strange world cold.

But Pilgrim Dusmano seldom went cold or unprepared into new lives or new earths or ecumens nowadays. His echoes, his coronal fields, his ripples were always going before him now. Wherever he went, there would be competent persons waiting to serve him, to organize for him, to build highways for his projects. And there would be intelligent young persons waiting to be instructed by him; aye, and waiting to set up cults in his honor.

These people had never truly heard of Pilgrim before. They did not really know him. They had not actually expected him. They would not recognize him. There wasn't any close kindred or accord. There wasn't any memory; there wasn't a call of like to like across a void.

But these people of several sorts had almost heard of Pilgrim. They had come very near to knowing him. They had been expecting, in expectations that did not put themselves into words, someone very much like him. And, while they did not exactly recognize him, they all recognized the thrill that his coming had brought to them. The specifications of that thrill of encounter had been implanted in all of them strongly. It had been enkindled in them in that infinity where parallel worlds meet.

It wasn't that there was very much to Pilgrim. He was a walnut with a small and tasteless meat inside. But it was recognized that he was of a rare and special species, and somewhere out of the encounter with him there would be a more ample and a nuttier harvest. And Pilgrim himself, whenever he arrived at a place, would stand on that shore and take hundredfold bread, dry and warm and savory and salted and wrapped in honey-wax, out of the water.

One of the high pleasures for Pilgrim Dusmano was the manipulating of minds, particularly the very plastic minds of the young. Pilgrim lived entirely for pleasure; that much must be understood about him. He hadn't any conscience; one who travels as often and as far as Pilgrim did must lighten his baggage of all such unessentials. But Pilgrim had so many possible pleasures tumbling around him at one time that he could select only the most exquisite of them. And moulding, sometimes eradicating, sometimes forcing, sometimes raping these minds and psyches and individualities—these things were exquisite to him.

Then, a little later every morning, after Pilgrim had tended to this particular horticulture, he turned his interest and activity to the areas called politics and manipulation and maintenance—or called nothing at all, though understood to be the main affair of the world. These things are important. They are the pivots that the world turns upon. And there is real enjoyment in them for one with a sufficiently spacious mind. Pilgrim Dusmano was a man who was intrigued by intrigue. All this interplay of world forces as weighed in human minds was the activating area that he would never willingly forgo. And the key man in Pilgrim's intrigues and governing was Noah Zontik.

The relationship between Pilgrim and Noah was on many levels. Sometimes Zontik looked at Dusmano with puzzled eyes. Scenes flicked past those puzzled eyes and were reflected in them. They were off-this-world scenes, out-of-mind scenes, out-of-context scenes. They were deep and abiding scenes of things that had happened far away and long ago. And (an awkward thing about them) they were scenes that had happened to other persons and not to Pilgrim Dusmano or to Noah Zontik.

How could distant and unremembered friendships between other men have such a reflection and near recollection in these two men in the present? Well, such things as had happened to parallel persons had perhaps very nearly happened to these two also. No, there had to be more to it than that.

Pilgrim and Noah had known each other for no more than a dozen years, but they were very much closer than this duration would suggest. Of the two, it would always be Noah who gave and Pilgrim who received: a clear arrangement. It was Pilgrim who always made or found advantage in that wide tangle of buckling, parallel worlds which he nearly, but not quite, remembered.

And, a little bit later yet every morning, after the political machinations (another word for "politics" is "survival"), Pilgrim Dusmano would go to attend to his commerces and businesses. This was the third most important thing for him. After providing for the future with young devotees, after securing the present with manipulated walls and alliances, Pilgrim liked to harvest his past plantings; this is what business and commerce consist of.

Pilgrim had a fabulous import business of wide ramifications and abrupt anomalies. One of the most stubborn of the anomalies of this business was in the case that, while Pilgrim Dusmano sold and delivered millions of dollars of commodities each month, he could not quite remember where he got the stuff he sold. And he could never recall whether he had paid for it, or how. A man who worried about such things would be in trouble, but Pilgrim didn't worry.

Really, on any world at all, there will be a great deal of such unusual commerce. A world couldn't get along without it, and it is never well to examine it too closely.

Pilgrim went to the headquarters of his businesses and enterprises now. He went to his main terminal with its shimmering and enigmatic floor. Some persons believed that this floor had the smell of bi-location. And Pilgrim was met there by a young man named Aubrey Pym. Aubrey was very nervous; indeed, his seemed to be an unaccustomed nervousness this morning.

"Ah, something new in nervousness," Pilgrim said with good nature. "I wonder, Aubrey, whether we could package it and create a market for it?"

"Mr. Dusmano, I want a raise in pay," Aubrey said in an ashen voice. "I have been thinking about it all night."

"I thought about it in the night also," Pilgrim said. "But for a short while only, not all night. It's the time of the week to send a messenger, and my intuition tells me that the messenger should be you."

"A messenger? Oh, that isn't my classification, sir. You thought about *me* and about my getting a raise? You thought about this last night?"

"Oh, yes."

"Well, I decided I would ask you as soon as I saw you

today. I want a raise. I know that I am clumsy in this, but—well, I have said it. I want it, Mr. Dusmano. I deserve it. I have been a good and faithful worker."

"Yes, I suppose so. What is it you have in your family, a wife and two children?"

"Yes, that's correct, Mr. Dusmano."

"Familied men make the best messengers. Built-in hostages, you know. They have something to carry through for. Other men may duck aside or simply die as the easiest way out of a situation sometimes. Men with families may try to duck, but they will find hands holding onto them. Well, bring your wife and your two children down here at once and we'll figure out the messenger role. Bring them from wherever they are. Then we will see."

"But the older child is in school at this hour, and the other one is in nursery school. And my wife is at her archery league this morning."

"Good. It's so much easier to find them when you know where they are. Bring them here, Aubrey. Then we will see about the raise and other things."

"But I don't quite understand."

"Don't you understand my words?"

"Yes, I understand your words, but not—"

"That's all that I want you to understand. Comply with them."

"Yes, Mr. Dusmano. All right."

Pilgrim went in to a board meeting then. Whenever he sat down to board with three or more of his employees it was a board meeting. He scanned the faces of the men who met with him. All these men had come to like Pilgrim. They were all very nearly entranced with him, but they were a very little bit afraid of him also. Somehow they had forgotten, over the years, that there wasn't very much to this Pilgrim man.

Well, who was the most afraid of him? Which of them was

C843995

the most nervous this morning? Pilgrim decided it was the associate named Spurgeon.

"All right, Spurgeon, what is it?" Pilgrim asked that man.

"Supply," Spurgeon said nervously. "There will have to be certain adjustments made in Supply. And you are the only one of us who knows anything at all about Supply. You are the only one who knows how to contact them."

Why should Spurgeon be nervous about bringing up this subject? It was brought up regularly every week, and it was dealt with efficiently every week. But this was one of the things that Spurgeon and the other leading men of the Commerce, great minds as they were, simply did not remember from week to week. Part of the difficulty was that Pilgrim insisted, at the end of every week, in burning the weekly minutes. There was a reason for it, he insisted, and someday that reason might be discovered. So now these men did not recall that the question of change or adjustment in Supply had ever risen before. They did not recall that the question was regularly solved. But everything about Supply was in a shadowy and quasi-forbidden area.

"It is only on my unconscious levels that I know how to contact Supply," Pilgrim said, "or else it is in some equally dark corner of my resources. For the fact is that I haven't any idea, any more than you have, where Supply is located. Well, draw up your recommendations, then; you, Spurgeon, and all of you. We've never had quite enough flexibility in the region of Supply, have we? And yet we've always gotten by. Let us make a transcript of what we want to convey, and I'll find the messenger to convey it."

"How will you find a messenger to go to Supply, Mr. Dusmano, since nobody knows where Supply is? What messenger can find the way? Have you a particular messenger in mind for this?" Spurgeon asked.

"Yes," Pilgrim told them. "The idea that we might need a messenger today came into my mind last night. I decided that we had an open place for a messenger. And the messenger himself, the one whom I had almost selected during a wakeful moment last night, came to me only a minute before I entered here. It will be a man and his wife and his two children, of course."

"Mr. Dusmano, I never quite understand about the messengers you send," Spurgeon said. "I had really forgotten, till this moment, that you do send them out often. I have a weak stomach, though, and I have the impression that there is something squeamish about the way you send them. And there is something really outré about those who arrive here."

"You were one of them who arrived here, Spurgeon, and it was less than a year ago," Pilgrim told him. "And you were as outré a messenger as any who ever came to us."

"Oh, well, I forgot then. I forgot how it was that I happened to come here. But as to the messengers and your sending them out, isn't there also something about their situations or families that you consider when you send them?"

"Yes, I never like to break up families, not when it would be forever," Dusmano told them. "And I try to send families of the typical size and shape that prevails wherever Supply happens to be located at that time. And I activate the members of the family to be strings on my messenger.

"Well, what is it that is wrong with the commodities that are coming from Supply? Is the sulphur in the handy-fuel too high or too low now? Is the structure-stock that we are receiving for the building industry too magnetic or not magnetic enough? Is the national barley that has become the bread of this world too bland or too sharp of taste this week? Is the proto-protein too agglutinative or too loose? Are we ready to try some of that comparatively new product that Supply has been suggesting to the under-minds of all of us for some time? Let us see if we can draw up a bill of particulars to take care of all recommendations for change in requirements for an entire week. For reasons that I hardly understand myself, it is difficult for me to send more than one agent to Supply in any one week. Can you gentlemen have a corpus of requests drawn up within one hour?"

"Yes, I believe we can," Spurgeon said, and the other high gentlemen nodded their agreement. They felt better and safer, now that Pilgrim seemed to know something about contacting Supply.

So Pilgrim Dusmano went out from the meeting room to give his men the opportunity of drawing up the instrument unspooked by his presence. He went out to pasture his always ravening mind in the green world outside. He maintained a fine parkland near his headquarters, and he walked in it now.

Pilgrim Dusmano was a handsome man, with contoured and flowing fair hair. He had a powerful and carrying voice, but at the same time it was intricate and modulated, almost feminine. He was a man who had just gone into early middle age, and he would have to call a halt to the aging process sometime before another decade had passed. He had a shimmer, a dazzle about him, or he made folks believe that he had such. He had been called, in the popular press, the hypnotic man, the electric man, the magnetic man, the transcendent man. Why should he not be called such things in the popular press? He paid men well to call him those things in that place. Praise is one of the primordial pleasures that can be bought for money, or for more tenuous barter. And genuine praise will often flourish after its synthetic foreshadow has delineated the way.

Someone was calling Pilgrim on his personal voxo. He accepted the call.

"Why did you kill Hut this morning?" Noah Zontik demanded of him, angry and exasperated.

"Who is Hut?" Pilgrim asked. He wasn't sure, but he could guess. He himself had killed only one man that morning.

"Hut is the cognomen of one of Evenhand's associates," Noah explained through the voxo. "He is a very important man, Pilgrim. He is much more important on his own than as an associate of Evenhand's. In Evenhand's group he is Hut, the shelter or the harbor, literally the hat. Why did you kill him?"

"He has been arrogant with me in the past, Noah, and it gives me pleasure to kill arrogant men. And Evenhand and his bunch have become very inquisitive about my doings. They will not even accord me privilege as a cult figure. If they want to play, then I will play with them. A cult figure needs a well-known group to be at war with him. Should I have killed a lesser man than Hut for my declaration of war? Killing Hut was my ante in the game."

"And if they stay and raise in the game (and they will), which one of us will they kill for the next action? You, Pilgrim, or me?"

"You to stay, me to raise. Preferably you, Noah, this early in the game. Possibly neither of us." Pilgrim doused his voxo.

Pilgrim Dusmano found Aubrey Pym with his wife and two children on the edge of the commodity arrival floor, that puzzling and shimmering area. All four of the Pyms were a little bit breathless and a little bit apprehensive. Pilgrim Dusmano was always a kind man, when being kind didn't interfere with his pleasure. But he believed that underlings were best kept a bit breathless and apprehensive. Apprehension was important in messengers especially; it was a key that fit many a door; it was often the only thing common to two worlds.

"Yes, I will give you the raise, Aubrey," Pilgrim said briskly now. "It will be a very substantial raise. And it involves a transfer for you, a transfer upward of course, a transfer to a whole new world full of opportunity. It will test you for all your ability. Do you think you can handle it?"

"Yes, yes, I will handle it somehow," Aubrey said. "I'll have acceptance and help in the new place, won't I?"

"Oh yes, every help, Aubrey. Should I send my people out cold?"

"We will transfer to another town?" Mrs. Pym asked avidly. "Oh, what town will it be, Mr. Dusmano?"

"How would I know?" Pilgrim said without thinking. And it didn't help much when he did think about it. How *did* he know such things, when he did know them? He stretched out the fingers of his intuition then as far as they would reach. "Dongolo, probably," he said. "Yes, I'm sure it will be Dongolo that you go to." However had Pilgrim come up with that name now? And however did he know that it was the true name? The names of the destinations, the details of the missions, all such things were usually barred from his mind. "You'll like it there, I know," he said.

"Dongolo? Is that the way you say it?" Mrs. Pym asked. "Isn't that where the Hemsteds went earlier this year? It will be good to see them again. But it's so far, isn't it? And we know so little about it. The people who go to those places must like them, though. They sure forget us fast when they go there, when they go to any of those funny-named towns. We never hear from any of them again after they go."

"Dispose yourselves correctly, you four," Pilgrim said. "It's absolutely necessary that you be in the right frame of mind for the jumping: apprehensive, nervous, determined, daring, creative in mind for the saving of your persons, defiant of the troubles of the trip, open to new things, yes, open like the gullets of lions. 'To be in the right frame of mind is a requirement for arriving at a new frame of existence'—that's a motto that we jumpers often use among ourselves.

"What? What am I talking about?" Pilgrim stuttered then. "Why did I say that last part of it? I've never been among jumpers at all. I don't know anything about their mottoes. I never even knew any jumper except myself. And why do I call myself a jumper? Come to think of it, I don't even know what I mean by a jumper."

"Neither do we," Aubrey Pym said uncertainly.

"But I bet we're going to find out," Mrs. Aubrey Pym said.

"The hard way," said the younger child.

Who would ever have suspected that the little clod could even talk?

"I have to go and get a document for you in a few moments," Pilgrim mused. "It seems that there is always a document of some sort involved whenever a messenger is sent out. It's like the 'papers' that always had to be rescued from the burning buildings in the old melodramas. But it seems also that there's a sort of haziness involved whenever a messenger is sent, as though there were something so outrageous about the manner of sending that the whole business had to be kept hazy and easily forgotten. I don't remember just what it is that I do when I send a messenger out, but *I will know,* for that moment at least, when the time comes for it. And that time will be coming very soon. I will do whatever is necessary for me to do then. I will try to do it when nobody is watching, in case I do it badly. All I remember about it at this moment is that it is a very grotesque act. I will go and get the document now, and I will bring it to the four of you. And then you four Pyms can go to your assignment."

"To Dongolo?" Aubrey Pym asked.

"Yes, I believe so," Pilgrim hazarded. "That has the sound of a right place."

The haziness had had a small rift in it when Pilgrim came up with that name. But now it closed in on Pilgrim as regarded name and destination and purpose. Clarity is a danger in all these sendings out. It must be replaced by a sort of embattled trust.

"How much of a raise am I going to get, Mr. Dusmano?" Aubrey asked.

"Oh, your salary will be doubled," Pilgrim said easily. "And your fringes, ah, they'll be like the bangled fringes on the jacket of a carnival girl!"

"Showy, but not cover much," said the smaller Pym child. Damn that little clod anyhow!

Pilgrim left the Pyms then and walked along the edge of the commodity arrival floor or area. This was of a very large extent. A great bulk of supplies arrived at this area every minute. Tons and tons, thousands and even millions of tons arrived there hourly. There were great quantities of fuel stuff and clothing stuff and foodstuff and building stuff, of all metals and minerals, of all chemicals and compounds, of all machinery and vehicles, of tonics and talismans. It was a great mass of freight really.

But nobody knew how it came there or where it came from. Pilgrim Dusmano should have known. This was all his commerce and his business enterprise. He owned it. He said that he could never quite remember where all this stuff came from. Almost he could remember, but not quite.

It may be that the stuff was always there, but unshaped or unnoticed, in air form or earth form or some form. And it may be that it was transformed or manufactured in place there, with the elements of it already in the ambient, and the force for the transformation generated by the slight displacement of two coincident worlds. Even a slight displacement of two worlds could generate incredible force. This is what a bright young student, attacking the problem as theory, at the behest of Pilgrim Dusmano, had come up with.

Well, if the material came from the ambient, and the force came from a slight displacement of two coincident worlds, why were messengers to Supply needed? Oh, they had to go to Supply to make adjustments in the pattern, the student said.

"May not the pattern also be of this world?" Pilgrim had

asked him. "May not the pattern be in our own ambient? Why should we have to draw it from another ambient?"

"No, no, only half of the pattern can be here. The other half must come from elsewhere. It is the slight displacement of two coincident worlds that generates incredible force in the line of creativity and shaping also. Half the pattern has to come from another world."

"What if it all came from here?"

"Then it would be altogether ordinary. It would be too ordinary for such creative results. Anyone could do it then, and you wouldn't become rich and powerful."

That was a bright young student, but most of the time Pilgrim could not remember quite what it was that he said.

The material certainly was not delivered here by any visible sort of vehicle or conveyor. Nor was it, apparently, rematerialized here as it might be at the end of a conventional teleportation sequence. If it was teleportation, then where was the receiver for it? There was no such energy provided or consumed as a receiver would have to have; at least such energy was not instrumented. The material and supplies all appeared as the result of "One Smooth Operation." Who can add to this what he does not know?

The commodity arrival floor appeared to be electric, a field force nexus. It appeared to be magnetic, a secondary fugaro vortex. It appeared to be gravitational and to have aspects of drag-world gravity. But the best instrumentation denied that it was any of these things.

Nevertheless, there *was* that startling, shimmering effect enwrapping the area at all times. Nobody could deny that. Bi-location kickback sometimes produces such a shimmering effect. There are other situations that produce this effect also.

The other great worldwide wholesalers, Jones and Cloud, Chung and Ching, Ivanova and McCresh, Izzersted and Panenero—each firm had its own "One Smooth Operation" for the reception of world supplies. But none of them had the same "One Smooth Operation" that Dusmano's Commercial Enterprises used. Pilgrim thought about these things. Then blind lightning struck.

In calm agenda of the day
Why should such mere dispatch be chilling?
A jeweled glance, five pints to pay,
A kid that took a lot of killing.

Commercial Messenger Weekly

Dusmano was struck down on the edge of the commodity arrival area. He received a body shock such as no man could survive unchanged. He was picked up again; then, like a stringy glob of wet clay, he was manhandled, he was secured, he was throttled almost beyond the point of death. He was shaking with the force of the onslaught; do dead men shake like that? Nobody jumped Pilgrim in his own place, not ever. Nobody struck him with such instant and silent power.

Dusmano was quite strong and active, a vital man. He was agile. He had imagination, he had spirit, he had heart. He had the old male courage, and he also had a few of the alien juices. He knew the repertoires of all the great personal-combat disciplines.

Pilgrim Dusmano was about as good an amateur scrapper as was to be found anywhere. But he was in the hands of a really remarkable man who had slipped up on him (and nobody slipped up on Dusmano ever), and who was handling him as if he were a child. Such men were not common. This man was certainly not an amateur, and just as certainly he had to be a known man. Pilgrim could have counted on the fingers of one hand all the men on that world who could have handled him so. Count this man on the fingers of one hand though and you'll get all your fingers broken.

"He is killing me with his hands," Pilgrim realized to himself in balanced panic. All Pilgrim's reactions and compensations were working well. That the man was killing him proved that he was not dead yet. That he was in panic proved that he had resources left. He drew what strength he could from his channeled panic and found that it was not enough.

"He is killing me with his hands," Pilgrim thought in a detached and lively-eyed despair, "and there is not yet anything that I see to prevent it. I cannot call out, for my throat is closed. I cannot twist. I cannot break away. He can snap my neck and kill me in an instant. He can shut off the rest of my breath and kill me in two instants. He can do these things; why hasn't he done them? Are the instants always as long as these when one is dying? I don't remember them that way."

Yes, there was something puzzling here. The final instants were too long.

"I'm not ready to die," Pilgrim protested to himself. "I cannot even gather my wits for a jump. Oh, oh, he's one of *those!* It will be a ritual killing. All to the bad, or all to the good, depending on how I can twist it. It will give me a little time to ready my mind for a world-jump. The jumpers have a saying that an unprepared death may cost one the advantage of two or even three lives. And the jumpers also have a saying about being on the wrong end of a ritual killing."

Pilgrim Dusmano prepared himself rapidly for his death and for his world-jump. He would salvage what he could. His assailant meanwhile had in hand what was probably the ritual knife, slender and sharp. The assailant had opened a vessel in the side of Pilgrim's throat, and the blood was flowing out. But it wasn't being wasted. It is hard to concentrate on an advantageous world-jump when a man is opening your throat with a ritual knife.

The assailant had a tankard. It was an old period piece with a flip lid. If it was ritual it was out of a hearty barroom ritual. The strong man was filling the tankard with Pilgrim's blood. And Pilgrim saw, with an inattentive flick of the eye (for his mind was occupied with the correct philosophy of world-jumping), that it was a five-pint tankard. That's a lot of blood to take out of a man at one time.

Pilgrim's hands were free most of this time. It was a measure of the attacker's strength that he didn't seem to worry much about the hands. But pounding on the trunk of that strong man was about like pounding on a petrified oak bole. Pilgrim could notice, from a slanted view of the man's large, lank, slab-sided face, that the man was very intense about something.

"Why should *he* be intense and passion-taken?" Pilgrim questioned himself in his dizzied and fading consciousness. "*I'm* the one whose life is in the balance. Still, if he is intense, then he is vulnerable somewhere. There's a saying that a chthonic demiurge will find work for idle hands. That mine be not idle!"

There was once a drowning man caught underwater who busied himself gorging on prime fish eggs. He liked them, and he might never have another chance of eating any of them, and he might as well have some advantage out of his predicament. Pilgrim busied his hands about the strong man's garments and trunk. Especially he busied one hand about a thing in the man's inner breast pocket. Pilgrim knew what it was as soon as his fingers touched it, but he had seldom come on so large or fat a one. Pilgrim removed the thing from the man's pocket and slipped it into one of his own, and that blood-drawing man was too intense even to notice it. "I'd fire that man if he were working for me," Pilgrim's flickering mind mumbled. "I don't care how strong he is. He shouldn't let himself be so easily distracted."

Pilgrim woke up (it couldn't have been much later; it had been only a short ritual sleep or death) on the flickering apron of the commodity arrival area. Sticky, red, syrupy blood stuff had stained the shimmering floor and set up a rejecting sputtering. Pilgrim put thumb and finger to the side of his throat and was almost able to stop the scarlet flow which had already declined greatly from its spate. The assailant was gone from the area, and so were at least five pints of Pilgrim's blood. Something had happened to Pilgrim, something a little bit more than his weakness. There had been a change in his eyes. It was as if they were really opened for the first time. Much brighter, but much more fractured; light poured in by them now. Waking with new eyes was almost the same thing as waking in a new world.

Pilgrim rose to his feet. Then he fell down in a dizzy faint. He repeated this several times. Then he got himself up and tolerably solid on his feet, and he walked. He cleaned himself a little in one of the ornamental fountains that were on the edge of the commodity arrival floor. Then he went into the board meeting room.

"We have almost finished the bill of particulars, Mr. Dusmano," Spurgeon said. None of the men paid much attention to the appearance of Pilgrim.

"All right," Pilgrim said. He sat down and examined the

wallet he had taken from the inner breast pocket of the unkilling, intense assailant. The men there may have thought their employer Dusmano had gone on some blood-for-health-and-happiness kick, if they thought about his appearance at all. The sparkling Dusmano, who was working very hard at becoming a worldwide fad, was himself a faddist of unlimited range.

First of all, there was a quantity of large-bill cash in the wallet. "My blood for drachmas," Pilgrim quipped to himself.

Then Pilgrim's fingers and eyes stumbled onto sudden knowledge while prowling through the fat wallet of the vanished assailant. Such information should never be carried on a man. "If he worked for me, I'd fire him," Pilgrim said once more. But this particular man, who behaved as though he could whip any man in the world—who may have been able to do so—had likely felt himself safe in carrying anything he wanted to carry.

Pilgrim, as soon as he had waked into dizziness on the apron of the commodity area, had remembered the public identity of the assailant. He had remembered it even though he had had no more than a very angled and blurred look at the big, slab-sided, intense face. Yes, that man, Mr. Holiness-through-Strength himself, really could whip any man in the world. Now Pilgrim learned, from a notebook in the wallet, the private or code or cognominal identity of this man.

He was one of the henchmen of that enemy Evenhand, and his code name was Mut or courage. And then, there in the middle of the doodles of the private man or the masked-man Mut, were written the code identities of all the henchmen of Evenhand:

Blut, who was blood or family.
Brut, who was the brood or spawn.
Flut, who was the flood, or the breaking-out, or the overflowing.
Glut, who was the blaze or flame.

Gut, who was the property.

Hut, who was the harbor or the shelter, who was also the hat
(and who was dead).

Mut, who was the courage (but not, apparently, the careful-
ness).

Wut, who was the rage or mania.

Was Evenhand's own code name given there? Oh, certainly. It was Rut, which is the rod or the scepter or the
authority. What? How big a boss was Evenhand, anyhow?
Was he the ruler himself?

Pilgrim remembered with real pleasure the man he had
killed that morning, Hut, who was the shelter or the harbor
or the hat. There had been eight of these assistants to
Evenhand (Rut). Well, why should such a devious octopus
have eight legs coming out of his central devil's head? And to
what man of the most secret and the most high office are
there appended eight secret and strong assistants? Pilgrim
guessed it. He was sure of it. And then he read it boldly
written down on another page. Now he knew who his enemy
Evenhand really was. He was the holder of the office like
none other in the country.

"I hadn't any idea that Evenhand was so *innocent* a man as
that." Pilgrim rattled this new thought around in his mind. "I
had no idea that he was so good a man as that, that he was so
absolutely spotless a man. But he has been certified so or he
would not occupy such office. Well, I hold no brief for
innocence or goodness or spotlessness. They have no more
than clinical interest for me. To think that I was once secretly
considered and weighed and investigated for that same
office. Well, they have it written down somewhere, in an
obscure but interesting corner of the national archives, that I
am not innocent, that I am not good, that I am not spotless.
It's good to have official, even if secret, confirmation of one's
own opinion of oneself. But I could have made a good thing
out of that job.

"But now I must find and join the concert of those who would bring down and destroy Evenhand. It is time to bring the movement out into the open and put it into effect. *There has to be* such an opposition movement. Really, the only reason for having men in that office is that they may be destroyed in that office. It is the ritualistic and satisfying scratching of a national itch, of a world itch. It will be the huge raping, the great gang-shagging. It will be a corporate pleasure almost without equal. It's so rich a satiation to topple giants, especially good giants."

Spurgeon and his fellow workers weren't quite finished with the bill of particulars to be sent to Supply. So Pilgrim still mused and schemed.

And halfway across town, Evenhand, a tall and slim man of mid middle age, had been nibbling at the agenda of both sets of his affairs: the open set, and the official and secret set. A man came in through a hidden door behind Evenhand, came in soundless and saturnine, and stood bulky and powerful behind Evenhand. Evenhand felt the power of the silent man, but he was not alarmed. It had to be one of eight men (seven live now, and one dead), for only one of those eight could possibly come through that hidden door.

"Who is it?" Evenhand asked, raising his head. "And what is it?"

"It's Mut," the powerful and bulky man said. "And about Dusmano, he bleeds red."

"Oh? Then he's probably human. So few real aliens are."

"Likely he *is* human. It's not certain, though. I don't believe he comes from any outer world, only from an aspect world. Here's a sample of him. Do you want me to get other samples from the creature? I could easily rip out lung tissue or brain tissue. Or the heart. It would be good to know whether it is two chambered or four chambered or six chambered. Or I could bring you the reins or the liver of the man."

"I don't want him killed, Mut. Not yet."

"Killed? No. I'd rip out the software so quickly as to leave him still writhing and alive. And then he would die within a few seconds in one of those unprovable effects of my cause. He would be dead, but could we call him killed?"

"You like that sort of stuff, don't you, Mut?"

"Certainly. You have to have someone attached to you who likes it. You yourself are spotless by definition. All that means is that your spots are externalized and localized. So they are. They are externalized in eight of us (seven alive and one dead now). And mostly these spots are externalized in me."

"We'll not kill him yet, Mut," Evenhand said. "I'm really sorry he's human. It's so hard to accept that a human can be so evil a person, so attractively evil a person. And our own job is to preside over an interplay of forces, and he's such a force. We interfere only a little. And we wait and watch."

"Yes. And then we are destroyed while we wait and watch too long."

"True, Mut, all too true."

"You want the blood, Evenhand? It has a good strong tang to it."

"No. I don't drink blood."

"I do sometimes," Mut said. And he drank off five pints of it in one big draft.

"It is finished, Mr. Dusmano," Spurgeon said back in the board meeting room. "It's really quite a routine paper. We draw up one like it every week, don't we?"

"I believe so, yes," Pilgrim said.

"Then why do we always forget that it's routine?" Spurgeon asked. "Why do we forget that it's a usual thing? Why do we always soup ourselves up into thinking it's a crisis event, instead of seeing that it's dull and almost automatic?"

"I believe it's because nothing with a dull and automatic

feel can be transmitted by the channels I must employ. There has to be a sense of urgency, or the message cannot go at all, and the messenger cannot. And when repeated urgency becomes routine, then memory failure must be intruded into it."

Pilgrim took the list, the bill of particulars, the requests to Supply for some slight modifications and additions to the flow of materials. He went out with the list to find the Pyms.

He found them looking uneasy. They were sitting on four long stone benches; beside them was a large material-grinder-and-shredder machine.

"Wherever did those things come from?" Pilgrim asked the Pyms and the world at large. "I didn't know we had any benches of that sort in stock. And that grinder-shredder is a model I don't recognize at all. Brrr, it's about the right size to be a people-grinder!"

"But the workmen brought these things here just a few moments after you left us, Mr. Dusmano," Aubrey Pym told him. "They said you had just then told them to bring these things here. They said you had them set up here about once a week. Isn't it all right?"

"Oh, yes, it's quite all right. I almost remember what they are for now. It's all coming to me with a rush, the ritual thing that I'm supposed to do. Is that really the only way we have of getting messages across the gap? It isn't good to know the ritual or to remember it between times. If I always remembered it, it would become stale. Here is the message, Aubrey. Hold it tight."

"Yes, yes. Nothing will get it away from me."

"Well, is everybody properly disposed for the journey?" Pilgrim asked.

"Yes, I am," said Aubrey Pym.

"Yes. We will all go together to happiness in a new town at double pay," the wife said.

"Yes," said the older child.

"No," said the younger child. "Hey, there's something wrong with your eyes." There was mockery in that child, and a bit of hate.

"Happiness and trust are essential," Pilgrim told the Pyms. "But do not let go of your apprehension. All of you lie down on your stone couches now. Did not the workmen bring a very large stone knife also?"

"Yes, there it is." Aubrey pointed.

"So it is," Pilgrim admired. He took it in his hand. "It fits me as though I had used it before. Stone is so ritual! Now, please, all of you set your thoughts on a bright and high and invisible bridge. This is a bridge that exerts a powerful charm. You are all going to cross that bridge to another world. But at the same time it will be the world that you are already in, seen in another aspect. It will be an aspect deplaced much less than a millionth of an inch from the aspect you are in now. Are all of you ready, in valor and joy, to cross this high bridge?"

"Yes," said Aubrey Pym.

"Yes," said his wife.

"Yes," said the elder child.

"No," said the younger child. "You have jeweled eyes. You didn't have them before. Maybe somebody will kill you and steal the jewels out of your eyes." There was really rampant mockery in the behavior of that child now, and there was much more than a bit of hate.

Pilgrim Dusmano quickly cut the throat of Aubrey Pym with the ritual stone knife. Aubrey rattled a bit in his cut throat and in his decapitated lungs. Then he died.

"That seems extreme," said the wife. "How is that going to get us moved to another town? Are you sure that's the way it's done?"

"I'm sure," Pilgrim said. "If I used a less grotesque method of sending messengers from this world, my competitors would be onto them in no time at all. Be well disposed, good wife. Be happy, but apprehensive. Be valiant."

"Oh, all right," the wife said. Pilgrim cut her throat with the ritual stone knife. She made sharp, windy sounds as if she wished to say something else. Then she died.

"Is it my turn now?" the elder child asked.

"Yes," Pilgrim mumbled, and he cut the child's throat with the stone knife.

"Can you use a new knife on me?" the younger child asked. "That one's dirty. You have jeweled eyes like a fly that's as big as a man."

"There's only the one knife," Pilgrim said. "Come now."

"Oh, no!"

And then there was absolute confrontation. The four-year-old child glared at Pilgrim with snake's eyes, with basilisk's eyes. There was agate fire in the eyes of that small and suddenly unnatural creature.

"I'm not going," the child sputtered. "You can cut my head clear off, but you can't kill me. You might be able to send me away from here, but I'm not going to go all the way to there. I'll hide in the passages and in the glaciers, and I'll trap you there the next time you have to travel. I'll be there where there's only room for me, and I'll knock you clear into hell when you try to pass. You'll be scared."

Somehow this way of speaking didn't match that of a normal four-year-old child.

"Your papa and your mama have already gone," Pilgrim said in false-ringing words. He never knew how to talk to children. Especially he never knew how to talk to precocious children. "Don't you want to go with them?"

"No. I want to stand on that narrow ledge and knock you off into hell the next time you come by. I know right where it is. I've been there before."

And Pilgrim Dusmano had one hell of a time cutting that

kid's throat. The child was slippery. It was sputtering and biting. It was cursing and foaming. And there were some inopportune workmen going by, and it made Pilgrim feel a little foolish to be killing a child while they gawked. Pilgrim always tried to dispatch messengers when nobody was watching. He finally cut the child's throat with very bad grace.

But the messenger-dispatching affair itself did not seem to be seriously flawed by this little unpleasantness. Pilgrim watched the words of the message fade from the paper that was still held in the dead hand of Aubrey Pym. And the fading of the words meant that the message had been received by Supply in the other world or in the other aspect.

And it also meant that the messengers, or three of them anyhow, had made a successful transition to another world or to another situation, that they were alive and well, that they were in parallel bodies in a parallel place.

This transition was all very routine. It was done every week with some messenger family. That is one of the ways messages are sent to other aspects by persons whose commerce is widely scattered. If it weren't for such setups, there would be no commerce at all between Present World and such places as Dongolo. And this established commerce, even though some of it might be invisible to persons of certain attitudes or situations, was always advantageous to both parties. It wouldn't have taken place otherwise.

The doors between different situations or worlds may be opened in peculiar ways such as this, but they may not be opened very wide or very often. And the knowledge of how they are opened cannot be left lying around. Even those who may sometimes have to use such means cannot be allowed to remember the trick of them.

So Pilgrim Dusmano was forgetting even as he stuffed the bodies into the grinder-shredder machine. He honestly did not recall how those bodies happened to be there. He knew they should be disposed of, and he disposed of them. But he found it all unaccountably distasteful.

He stuffed in the big male body and sent it, sloshing in its own juice, to its reduction. Then the big female body went in. And then the little male body. And then the little—well, what was it, anyhow? Pilgrim was damned if he knew the sex of that smallest creature, and he was damned if he cared. The meat of it was still hot, and perhaps it was still making defiant sounds in its severed gullet. Was it taken by death then, or merely by a purple pout? Pilgrim stuffed it into the machine.

But a moment later, as Pilgrim glanced at the final stage of the disposal, he saw that one hate-shot, child-sized eye was riding the remaining effluvium of the people-grinder. There was no doubt that the eye was conscious and that it was glaring at Pilgrim with bottomless hatred. That child could yet make trouble!

Pilgrim Dusmano turned his back on it all and forgot it. Workmen came and removed the four large stone benches and the long ritual stone knife. As soon as it had completed its reduction process, the grinding machine was also removed by the workmen. And these things were put away for another week.

One week hence, Pilgrim Dusmano would see these objects again, and he would not remember that he had ever seen them before. Only when it came time that he must use them would he remember what it was that he must do with them.

5

An idol-thing with jewel eyes
And kindness' milk grown thicker, curder,
With tampered shadows, Scanlon skies,
And token, microcosmic murder.

Museum-Munchers' Daybook

Unrepeated information goes stale quickly. It festers. Pilgrim Dusmano had acquired certain information that morning from the wallet of the man with the code name of Mut, so he felt himself compelled to pass it along, unfestered yet, to places where it would do the most harm. He called, by voxo, a multimedia reporter named Randal Muckman.

"What I have is too hot for voxo," he said simply. "Muckman, if you can be coming out of the Daylight Museum in four minutes, I will pass you as I go in. And I'll give you something."

Four minutes later, Pilgrim Dusmano, going into the Daylight Museum with jaunty and innocent step, passed Randal Muckman coming out.

"Evenhand is Consul," Pilgrim said in a quick, low voice; and almost instantly there were many steps between the two men. It was as quick and easy as that. But was ever such explosive information compacted into three words! If the identity of a Consul were known, then the government of a land or a world would be in perilous straits.

Could Muckman believe what Dusmano had just told him about his known enemy? Dusmano wasn't known at all for his honesty. What he was known for was the sheer variety of his dishonesties. But why should anyone pass along such rotten information? Why do it, if it were false? Why do it even if it were true? Just for the steep pleasure of it, perhaps, in the case of Dusmano. He was widely known as a pleasure man, and he did get pleasure from imaginative defamations.

But how should Muckman tag the source if he did pass the information along? He had to pass it along or he wouldn't be Muckman. "From a usually unreliable source" would start the finger pointing in the direction of Pilgrim Dusmano. "From a knowledgeable man whose dishonesty few doubt" would have the scent of Pilgrim all over it.

Six minutes later Muckman did go on the tinsel with his hourly items and gave the information as "From a high, wide (of the mark sometimes), and handsome source." At least the more intelligent and more current people knew that the source had to be the devious Pilgrim.

The three-dimensional eddies from the shocking report quickly swept over the whole land. That anyone should reveal the identity of a Consul still in office was pretty raw. So Dusmano had already done the first stage of his damage. He gloated fast, that man, and then he went on to other pleasures—to the building of a particular image, his own.

The Daylight Museum, where Pilgrim now fatted his mind

for an hour on the plain abundance, was based on the concept of art at its best, uncompromised and untrammeled. "It's always nice to provide the brackets where the trammels can be hooked on later," Pilgrim had said one day. But there were no dark corners in the Daylight Museum. And there were no dark concepts there. There were no abstractions. If a person wanted abstractions, then let him draw them out himself, from the clear material here, and from his own mentality and psyche. If a person wanted murkiness, then he could fashion it himself, but it should not be second-hand murkiness. The original representations in this museum must be clear, both in line and in thought. And the colors should be chaste. There was a rule that there should be no color which a sane mind and a clear eye cannot view without a fever rise of more than four points, or without the unease index exceeding seventy-five over sixty-two. That was one of the basic rules at the Daylight Museum, and it was a good rule. It kept out certain sorts of junk.

(Pilgrim Dusmano had been busy creating a special image by every art he could lay hold of; it was partly for that reason that he frequented museums.)

The Daylight Museum did *not* have something for every taste. If a person wanted to view unruly pictures or statuary or transfixes, then he could go to the Dismal Den on Third Street, or to the Implosion House downtown, or to Tom Fool's out along the parkway. There were museums for every sort and taste. Even if a person had a taste for his own bloody tongue, he could go to the Introspection Inn on Frankfort.

(Just what *was* the special image that Dusmano was creating? Oh, it was just the image of his own ideated self.)

If a person wanted to experience the hot and dizzy and nauseous stuff, then let him go to hell (out in the Southgate complex). Pilgrim Dusmano tried to visit the several very different museums in the several days of the hebdomad. He didn't actually go to hell to encounter the dingy and nauseous stuff, but in Southgate Hell or the Dismal Den or Sheol Shuckins he often observed the very expensive sets of crockery that had been made out of swamp-born, plasticene-gray clay and had been slacked and fired in hell itself. And he saw other obscure things that had been in hell literally. None of those things were very artistic, but they were all passionate and powerful mood pieces. A person could become extremely moody just looking at them and handling them.

But today Pilgrim was enjoying his late morning hour at the daylight-infused Daylight Museum. He was joined there by Mary Morey ("Your eyes look funny today," Mary said, "like cracked glass or jewel. Your first breakthrough to a new image, and it's broken glass"), who was one of his early morning students. Pilgrim was now joined at very many things by Mary Morey. And, at the same time, he was not quite joined by another of his morning students, Mary's brother James Morey. James very often hung on the edge of Pilgrim's company, holding back in the shade, smiling, watching, listening. "Mary in the sunlight, James in the shadows" was a saying that some of the other students had about them. It was said by some, only partly in jest (experiments had actually been run on the thing, but mind-boggling happenings had always flawed the results), that Mary had no shadow at all except her brother James.

"How did you get new eyes?" Mary asked Pilgrim now. "Can anybody get new eyes?"

"Yes," Pilgrim said. When the man Mut had struck Pilgrim down that morning, Pilgrim had seen stars and jewels and pinwheels. But these bright things, after their moment of shine, didn't scatter and disperse at large. Rather they came together, and they came to lodge in Pilgrim's eyes. That was the way it had seemed, at that moment, to Pilgrim's reeling wits. Or the new eyes might have come about otherwise, but they did come about at the time that Pilgrim was struck down. The shattered eyes were connected with some shattering experience.

Mary cast a strange shadow, her brother. And also there was something unusual about the shadows that Pilgrim Dusmano cast. Those shadows would change even when Pilgrim did not change or move his position. They would change even when the light did not change. Whole parades of shadows, all of Pilgrim's casting, would follow one another. And the man Pilgrim would be passive, his eyes slitted (scatter-lit and occluded was the case with his new eyes) with interior pleasure, projecting the quick shadows out of his breathing body. The shadows may have been prime, and the fleshed Pilgrim may have been derivative. One fleshed shadow is easier to posit than that all those snapping lively things were the shadows.

"What is the matter with Mr. Dusmano?" Mary Morey asked the museum curator. "What is the matter with his shadows?"

"He exteriorizes badly or unevenly," the curator said. "That's the most simple way to put it. He is a pleasure seeker in all things, but for balance he pushes it too far. There's a lot of raw bloodiness associated with his pleasures. Where else would those red tinges in all his shadows come from except from his involvement in bloodiness? I suspect he's insane, but I believe he can leave off being insane anytime he wishes. It's a case, though, where he will set aside a special half hour here, an hour there during the day in which to enjoy his insanity. It's a part of his planned pleasures. So are you a part of them, young lady."

(A wave of excitement and emotion was going through the city, through the nation, through a good part of the world during those moments. It was a murderous, but pleasantly murderous, emotion, like killing an enemy in a dream. The waves of that excitement came through the very walls of the museum building and of every building.)

Pilgrim's shadow at that moment was a blob of high-hearted and intensely sociable evil. It was sociable in that every person present shared the dangerous attraction of that shadow. And the shadow was highlighted by a dance of red flute notes. But Pilgrim himself was gazing at a squarish, plain, black and white drawing of a boy and girl who were standing apart and doing nothing at all. The simply drawn girl was done in black on a sheeny white area. The scantly detailed boy was drawn or painted in flat white in the black halving of the drawing.

Then why should there be such shrillness in Pilgrim's own shadow? Possibly Pilgrim was abstracting from the sharp-line drawing. But why was there that high pitch to the red flute notes that were scattered about on the floor? The notes were too shrill to be heard by trammeled ears. They were so shrill that if there had been a glass there, it would have—but there *was* a glass there. And it shattered from the pitch of the shadow flute notes.

"I'm sorry," Mary Morey told the museum curator. "I feel that I was partly responsible for that. I hadn't seen the glass at all. That glass that was on exhibit on the table there, the curious glass that shattered, was it very valuable?"

"No. It was my drinking glass," the curator said.

"Dusmano enjoys himself." Young James Morey was speaking out of the shadows. "But does he have any fun out of his enjoyments and pleasures? His enjoyments might not be the same as fun. His pleasures are pleasurable by his own definition and that of his cult, but it's all a very taut thing. I'm part of it, and I don't know whether it's fun or not."

The museum curator had Dusmano into his reserved wardroom and showroom then. The Moreys were allowed to follow. There were several striking new arrivals at the museum.

"We have a few excellent new things on loan from

Melchisedech Duffy's Walk-In Bijou in New Orleans," the curator said.

Some of these new things were strident and some of them were serene. There were paintings, there were woodcarvings, there were German silver montages. And there was a little wooden statuette that had live eyes. It was by Groben.

The eyes of it were live and lively. They snapped. They crackled. There was a world of curiosity in them, and only the slightest edge of animosity. They were small brown monkey eyes; or they were small brown kobold eyes. Nothing else about the statuette was alive. It wasn't even a very good-looking carving, not for Groben.

"That little statue has live eyes," Mary said, "and they look like the eyes of somebody I know. And you, Pilgrim Dusmano, now that you have eyes that are dead and made out of jewel, don't you have idol-eyes now?"

"Yes, of course I have. And I'm in the way of becoming an idol."

"And has this little statuette acquired your old eyes, your live eyes? They look like yours. The statuette looks like you."

"I intend to make myself look like a statue, but not like a statuette," Pilgrim said. "But my old eyes shouldn't be alive anywhere. I'll not allow them to be.

"Let's drown it!" Pilgrim cried against the wooden statuette with an almost leprous interest. (Unspotted in his pleasures Dusmano was not.) "Ah, there is a fine ornate crock right there, James. Go fill it with water and drown the thing."

James Morey took the crock and went to fill it with water.

"Don't do it," the curator said. "We don't know the trick of the eyes yet. And dunking or drowning it might damage the mechanism."

"There isn't any mechanism," Pilgrim told them. "There is only a little wooden statuette with live eyes, and I recognize against all reason that they're mine. Ah, here you are, James. 'Fast as a shadow,' they always say about you, and it's so. Now just put the little carving into the water and hold it under."

"For how long?"

"Hold it under water until it is drowned. Or until we are weary of the micromurder. I pray that I may never be weary of such! Or until it is time for us to leave here for other pleasures."

James Morey put the little wooden statuette into water and held it under.

"What is the first requirement of a stone block, of a log, of a rough stock for the making of a statue or an icon or a—well, something more alive?" Pilgrim was asking. "What one quality would be most wanted in the blank or the wood or the marble or the clay or the—well, or the blank flesh?"

"That it be completely empty of real personality," the curator said. "If an unshaped block of stone shows personality, then it is worthless to an artist. If even a stretched square of canvas shows personality, then it will not accept art."

"Oh, well, I've nothing to worry about in my own case, then," Pilgrim said.

The fact was that Pilgrim Dusmano had been constructing, for a long time now, a statue or an icon or a—well, something more alive. He had been working carefully on this image, and he had put others to work on it also. There was work being done toward it in canvas and wood and marble and clay. But also, and mainly, the statue or icon or image was being made out of flesh—Pilgrim's own.

And the blank material for the image had indeed been empty of real personality. That allowed a clearer field to work in.

There was in that wardroom or showroom a fine, newly arrived, slightly larger than life-size wooden cigar-store

Indian by Finnegan. It was one of the most anomalous, one of the most woodenly vital things that Finnegan had done. And nobody else had ever carved cigar-store Indians like Finnegan. In its mahogany-colored wooden hand the Indian held a clump of very real-looking cigars. Real-looking? No, they were real. Pilgrim took four of the long stogies out of the clump and passed them around. And they all lit up.

"I never noticed that the cigars were real," the curator said, "but the Indian arrived only this morning, and I hadn't nearly finished looking at it. Yet I'm nearly certain that they were wooden cigars when first I looked. One of the workmen must have played a trick there. An expensive trick, though. These are very fine cigars: very fruitily cured; and very old."

"They're not from this century," James Morey said. Mary Morey was blowing heart-shaped smoke rings. She could flute her tongue in odd ways to form the various shapes in smoke. It's one of the lesser-known fine arts.

"I believe that the first thing one should do when setting to work on a rough, empty-of-real-personality stock or log or stone is to fill it with living blood," Pilgrim said. "That's what I've been trying to do. And I believe that as much blood should be poured on the outside of it as on the inside." Pilgrim's jeweled eyes glittered.

There were two Adam Scanlon seascapes there in the room. They were good. But it was as if those seas and the skies over them belonged to slightly different worlds than our own, or to our own world a long time ago.

A man brought in a written note and gave it to the curator. Then the man left.

There was a breath-flubbing triptych there. It was titled only *Dotty*. It showed on the left wing a girl clothed and pretty; in the center was the same girl unclothed and still pretty; on the right wing was the same girl shown cut away or visceral in the torso, and still pretty, even in the viscera. The triptych was signed by "Joe Smith" on two of the three panels. The third panel was not signed; part of it was painted in a different hand. This triptych was almost too good, and almost too nostalgic of something, to be believed. It wasn't the sort of thing one comes upon in every lifetime.

"If things like this come from the Walk-In Bijou in New Orleans, I wonder what else is there?"

"Very little to be seen," the curator said. "Melchisedech puts out trash and keeps the good stuff stored away in a lumber room behind."

There were four paintings by the mysterious Gregory van Ghi, whose works were all suffused with such an unworldly, ghostly orange color. It was as though a full moon had broken and been spilled over everything that van Ghi did. There were some who maintained that van Ghi had been a disciple of Finnegan. But van Ghi had been the older.

There were three Chicago-period wood-texture paintings by Alessandro, who—

"Ah, the note that one of my men has just given me," said the curator, "—it says that Evenhand is the Consul. It just came over the news."

"We'll hound him, we'll rend him, we'll tear him to pieces," Pilgrim cried out with real excitement. "We'll ruin him, we'll destroy him, we'll kill him and dismember him, and then we'll befoul his nest and his ashes."

"Why, Mr. Dusmano, why?" the curator asked in shocked puzzlement. "I could never understand the avidity of a whole nation for the destruction of a Consul. The Consul does fill the highest and most worrisome of jobs, without pay, without thanks, and in total anonymity. And he must be a good person and be certified as such. Why should a populace want to murder and destroy him?"

"It's the devil-revel, curator," Pilgrim howled. "It's the pleasure that comes hardly twice in a generation. It's the murder that a whole nation can take part in and enjoy and remember. It becomes a main part of our national heritage, of our world heritage. Curator, we kill him because he is Consul. And because he is a known man now and is vulnerable to be destroyed. And because it is almost the most burning pleasure of them all to destroy a marked person utterly. The ritual hounds must be set to howling and baying. And it is particularly a pleasure to destroy a high person if he is good. 'It is more pleasure to kill one good man than a hundred indifferent men'—is that not what the Louden Devil said? This is folk-knitting to form red history."

"The little wooden statue is being pretty nervous underwater," James Morey said. "It's hard to hold him down. He's in panic."

"It is only a wooden statue," the curator said.

"It is not only a wooden statue," Pilgrim Dusmano contradicted. "It's more than that. If it were no more than a wooden statue, would I be excited over its drowning in a state of panic? This micromurder will become a sauce for the big feast that we'll make on the body of Evenhand the Consul." Pilgrim glittered and glowed like a bonfire.

"I never understood it," the curator said. "My father tried to explain it to me. They destroyed a Consul in his time. But I never understood it."

"That's because you're a spotless sheep yourself!" Pilgrim barked in savage derision. "I hate your unrotted mutton! I hate any unspotted flesh! There may be a way to destroy you as a partisan of the Consul."

"I'm not sure I'd care," the curator said sadly. "If a good man is destroyed to death by a perverse world, I'd as soon leave that world too. But why, when there are so many evil men about, should there be this hysteria? For I can feel just that; I can feel it coming through the walls. Why should there be this hysteria to torture and to annihilate one good man?"

"Where's the fun in raping a harlot?" Pilgrim asked. "No, no, it has to be a completely innocent victim. It is the bruising and abusing of virgins to death that is such high pleasure. You are an art curator and you do not appreciate the high and pleasant art of this?"

"Why, why do people still do it?" the curator still croaked. "I feel them going for it now. I feel them going for it in every place in the nation. But it is insane. It is irrational. It is unnatural. What has gone wrong with the people?"

This curator was straight corned mutton.

"The people! The people know not how to distinguish between their right hand and their left," Pilgrim sneered. "Fortunately we have instant agitators, slashing wolves, dialectical experts. They are wild, ravening, and direct persons, unorganized on the visible plane, and with hearts ready for every rampant pleasure. They pour the words, they pour the instigations, they pour the enlivening action into the people; they pour it into all the senses and all the intuitions. They become the churning blood of the bloodless people; they are the deviled brains and the spastic spleens and the goatish gonads. What, should the people forget that they have hackles? Should they disremember that their hands must be red in the red season? Should they ignore what pleasure-music there is to be discovered in an agonizing death cry? We will not let the people forget! We will force the people to partake of the strong pleasure. We will pour it all into them. And in their ignorance they will respond to it. We pour it in now."

"I wonder what Judas it was who revealed the identity of the Consul!" the curator moaned, feeling the thin anger that even meek men sometimes feel.

"Judas, indeed!" Pilgrim was all glee. "I wonder what those other eleven idiot sheep found that was as good as the red-murder rapture and the self-murder exultation that the real Judas-goat knew!"

"It is like a Greek tragedy," the curator mumbled. "It is stark evil coming on goat feet. It is the tragos-goat himself. And he is the devil."

"Certainly, certainly," Pilgrim said briskly. "It is almost overflowing already. It animal-nickers. It bloody-bleats."

"The statuette is screaming underwater," James Morey said in his shadowy excitement. "It's so small, and there's a whole world in its screaming. I hear it with my fingertips. I wish you could hear it."

"I heard it," said Pilgrim, "and I enjoyed it all the way to the hot handle itself. With these things it is always the question of which alternative gives one the most pleasure. Should we enjoy the more and gloat the most over the swift death of the victim, or over the slow death? But you are wrong, curator. This is not a Greek tragedy of which we have gone through the first chorus and now begin the action. It is a Greek Katastrophy or destruction or ruination. It's a much more pleasurable thing than a tragedy. What is that which you take from your desk, curator? It interests me."

"It's the eyepiece from the ritual mask of the Consul who was destroyed in my father's time," the curator said.

"It looks like one of the new cracked-glass, jewel eyepieces in your own ritual mask, Pilgrim," Mary said. "You know that you now wear a ritual mask instead of a face?"

"I know it," Pilgrim said.

The Consuls were always elaborately masked and swathed and gauntleted while they fulfilled their offices. The Consuls were a series of absolutely good men who worked anonymously and masked upon the earth, undertaking to head up the governments. They made the necessary decisions from behind the veil, as it were. Even when they spoke, in their official and disguised capacity, they had to have a glottle in the mouth to trammel the tongue and disguise the speech. And the masked-Consul system had worked when it seemed as though nothing in the world would ever work again. Rulers had been assassinated so swiftly that rule had disappeared. And then the masked-Consuls had tempered anarchy enough for the world to continue. But if a Consul's face should ever be seen or his Consul-name should ever be spoken, then he would be known and marked, and he would be destroyed. The devils have the power to seize and dismember an unmasked man.

"Yes, the eyepiece is of polarized shape," Pilgrim said. "A man could see out of it, and nobody could see into his eyes. The eyes of this particular Consul were burned out with hot spits after he had been unmasked. Part of the smokiness of that event was said to have gone into the eyepieces of the mask. I wish I might have taken part in all that."

The cigar-store Indian was standing up in the middle of that room in all its unbending woodenness and angular morality. It was really the only moral person there. Pilgrim was not a moral person. The Moreys were not. Even the curator was not quite. The curator was fearful, and at the same time he was drawn to the blood-magnet.

"What was a Greek Katastrophy?" the curator asked in an itching voice.

"Oh, it was the assault, the sack, the rape, the ruin, the destruction." Pilgrim ticked the things off. "It was much more vital and much more dramatic than the arena games the Romans played. And it could be played out, passioned, dramatized, agonized, by large or small groups. In its classic form, mostly at Corinth, but other places as well, the victim had to be a virgin, male or female. And this victim had to be assaulted as many times as were required to bring it to death's gate. It was often a three-days-and-nights agony. Then, when the victim had arrived at the extremity, with body clear burst open and ripped apart, and with death howling and gibbering nearby, then every sort of torture was to be applied at once; and all sorts of people, even grandes dames and graybeards and small children, had to be brought to the assembly to add their own species of torture.

"The limbs would be broken clear off the still-living body.

The eyes and privates and tongue and glottis were torn clear out by their bloody roots. Oh, we live in a weak age that has forgotten the ancient pleasures! I was born too late and in the wrong place. We organize groups now and we do these things, but they are artificial. The spontaneity is lost. The genuine chthonic roots have shriveled, and they must be restored. Of course, if the victim were not a virgin, the difference would be felt at once. The pleasure simply would not be so rich."

"And the killing assaults on unmasked Consuls are analogous to this?" the curator asked.

"Yes, they are national solidarity acts," Pilgrim said. "They are the rich, ritual murders to renew our blood. But if the Consul were not really a good and spotless man, the difference would be felt from the first. The corporate murder-pleasure would not be so rich in that case. Fortunately, Evenhand really is spotless, so the uproar will have its full meaning and its rich, rancid pleasure. Such acts as ours can make the very spheres boggle. You know that.

"How is the carved wooden figure, James? Ah, it is our token lust and our token murder."

"We will see," James Morey said. He took the wooden figurine out of the water. The wood limbs had moved and redisposed themselves, though it wasn't a jointed figure. The members were displaced and deformed and distorted from the killing water-torture. The eyes were open and dead, but they were dead in horror and torture and desolation. The wooden drowned thing would almost have moved one to pity, had not one already decided to move in another direction. It was one of the strangest and most haunting little woodcarvings that Groben ever did.

"The eyes of it were the last remnant of the real Pilgrim, and now they're dead," James Morey said flatly. But James, however much he understood that Dusmano was making himself devilishly artificial, was still a leading member of the Pilgrim Dusmano cult.

Eclectic outrage is our rule:
To strain at gnats that soil and sin us,
And pass huge camels to the stool.
And *still* there are great camels in us.

"Song of the Golden Shovel"

Pilgrim Dusmano had midday dinner at the Media Club. He was an honored member of that body. Even the forbidding words written in flame over the entrance of the Club, "For the Lords Spiritual Only," were no obstacle to him. Pilgrim was a Lord Spiritual as well as a Lord Temporal. By his commerce and his money-shuffling he was a high Lord Temporal. But in his influence on mores and manners, on cults and quackeries, on modes and styles, he was a Spiritual. In his creative deviations and his decadent deformations, in his riotous dismantlings and numinous ambivalences he was a Lord Spiritual. And as a high "Pioneer of Pleasure" he was a certified Lord. For his scatterfield philosophy, for his promulgating of dynamic rutting as a fine art, for his kinetic taste and vectored variances, he was a real Lord Spiritual, bemedaled and cultified.

The Media People needed such persons as Pilgrim. And he, empty of real personality and interested in acquiring the finest cultic and electronic personality in the world, needed the Media. The production of such as himself, the chopping down of uncultic and unelectronic persons, that was what the Media had been all about for a long time, and that was what Pilgrim Dusmano consisted of. He was the Newest of the New Men.

A younger Lord Spiritual, one of the tinsel group of communicators, came to Pilgrim at table there. "We have uncovered and unraveled the three men, Gut and Blut and Flut," this young Lord said. "We have nailed their hides to the barn door, as the ancient saying has it. And we have published their names and faces for all to see and hear. 'Plague-Rats behind the Masks' is the way we label them. Unmasked they die! Nothing can save them. Who would want to save them? They are the unelectronic people, the nontinsel people, the folks of the unfractured flesh, and they never showed a deep love for us of the Media.

"Blut has already been killed. The people got to him before we had hardly started on our instigation. It was almost too easy. They tore him to pieces."

"Good." Pilgrim laughed with smacking pleasure. "Blut was a minor one, but we will quickly come to the main. What a pleasure-filled exit for me this will be!"

Pilgrim, a studied expert of innovative foods, was eating pipe clay soup, which is made of the vermicules that burrow into that white clay. The soup has naught else except Holland onions and a salting of the white pipe clay itself.

"And, Mr. Dusmano—" the young Lord began, with the hint of rich secrets.

"Yes, Cordcutter, the people tore Blut to pieces?" Pilgrim gave him his attention. "And then?"

"We have one of the pieces of Blut here, Mr. Dusmano. Here at the Media Club. And a fairly large piece it is."

"Oh, sweet, sweet! How long until?"

"Within the hour."

"Good. I'll dawdle and I'll wait. Oh, good!"

"Mr. Dusmano—" Cordcutter, the young Lord, began to ask, and other young Lords were interested. "These things do not open out of themselves. And you are always a source of information like no other. Give us our momentum again. Have you not some further piece of activating information?"

"Oh, yes. Mut is Satterfield." Pilgrim liked throwing that strong man to these strong-tooths.

"What, old Transcendent Muscles Himself is one of the masked men? Old Strength-in-Serenity? Oh, the public will rend him! There has to be something to get him for. Something, many things."

And the young Lords swarmed out like a cloud of gnats. Somewhere they would find or fake or manufacture the gnat of evidence against the great strong man, Strength-in-Serenity, Strength-in-Purity, Satterfield, who was now revealed as the man behind the code-mask, Mut. Always the Lords could find a gnat's-weight of evidence against any man, and always that gnat's-weight would be enough to declare ruination.

Were they Lords of the Gnats for nothing? Many of these young Lords Spiritual had already scattered to hunt down and hamstring this strong man.

For a people, even a good people, do not pass gnats easily, once they have gotten inside them. They will huff and puff and strain and turn purple, all over one adolescent gnat. And the gnat must be dissected, minutely dissected before it can be passed. It would never go out all in one piece. This selective passing is an oddity about even good people. They can pass out easily many very large objects, not to mention camels.

Pilgrim was eating mock-pizzle pie now, the genuine pie being out of season. But the mock pie was good, it was prestigious, it was expensive. The basic ingredient was from the clutter-buck rather than from a bull, but ah, it was an open secret that some of the most current people ate the mock-pizzle pie by preference even when the real thing was in season. Joy at board! What can unjade a jaded appetite like mock-pizzle pie!

An older and more elegant Lord Spiritual came to Pilgrim then. This was a man of fine appearance and distinction, and he bore the old and noble family name of Fairfronter. He wore the rare "Golden Shovel Pip" as a mantle brooch. But he also wore the even more rare "Pilgrim Staff" which was smaller than a mote in the eye. It was seldom recognized, even by the heraldry experts, what the small Pilgrim Staff was and meant. What it meant was that the bearer belonged to Pilgrim Dusmano and his cult, that he worked always to establish the Pilgrim image and cult.

"Is it final that you will leave tonight, Mr. Dusmano?" the Lord Fairfronter asked with anxious pain. "This world just won't be the same without you. Even from a purely technical point of view, you have advanced the posthuman personality beyond any others. But why do you leave so soon? Your cult has not yet outdistanced the others. Like all fine things, it takes its while to rise above the coarse growth around it. And when you do leave, whom will we look to for our leader? Have you nominated a replacement?"

"A replacement for myself, Fairfronter? Who but a further me could succeed me? Yes, it is final that I leave tonight, unless—well, unless I get some different notion. We intuitive ones know that times and directions are never final. Oh, as to appointing a leadership for those whom I leave behind, I can always send instructions back to you here.

"It may be yourself who will receive those instructions and play the leader. Could you be the burning voice and hands and body in lieu of myself? Could you represent the electronic-anointing in place of me? I build my system on world after world, and I leave my worlds shining behind me like the trail of a snail or a slug. I span those worlds with my personal celestial body. And this digesting of world power and world experience is as much internal to me as it is external. Each time I open a new world or a new stage of my life, it is like coming onto a never-before-noticed portal in my inner being. I open it, and I come upon a whole new rich suite of rooms already prepared for me in my interior.

"I suspect that the worlds really live in me and not I in them. My personal and cultish indwellings are as varied as they are rich. Really, I can never get enough of me. And always I can, wherever I happen to be, cut the throat of a human calf or a human sheep and send him back, or forward or anywhere, with a message. But my message will be the same burgeoning message forever: 'Don't think. Scintillate.' Thought is one mental process that must be excised out of us. There are so many patterns of mind that are better than thought."

"Is it possible that such dingy madness can really be of effect?" the man Evenhand, who was the unmasked Consul and who had the code name of Rut, was asking. He could listen anywhere. He did not entirely despise electronic or postelectronic technology. And he had been listening for a small moment to Pilgrim Dusmano. "Lords of the Gnats indeed they all are, and he is the slightest of them. For that reason, I suppose, he will become their mad king. Until finally he returns to his own place."

"I should have killed him this morning," Mut said, "but it

wouldn't have mattered. They are fungible, interchangeable, and there are so many of them. There is no limit to the articulating of artificial personalities, and Pilgrim has at least attained a certain cohesion that a quick substitute might lack. Yes, such dingy madness really *is* of effect, Evenhand, in our temporal vales. Every world that collapses does so by such a dingy madness eating out its brains and substance."

"Our faith commands us to love the sinner and hate the sin," Evenhand said, "but does it command us to love a reticulated mechanism that grinds out sin like sausage? Yes, I suppose it does. That mechanism of a Pilgrim, except for—except for being himself, could have been human."

"But I have lately begun a new and improved practice of taking my own place when I leave," Pilgrim was saying back at the Media Club.

"What? How do you mean it, Mr. Dusmano?" Fairfronter asked.

"Why, I'm a bundle of sticks, Fairfronter. I'm a million long and skinny sticks bundled together. Each person is something such, though I doubt if anyone has so great a variety as myself. The sticks are my parallel persons. No one person, no one stick, not even the one here present at table, can be a very great part of me. But when I go, I can always send another self after me as Paraclete. Every parallel of me is truly myself, but we cannot see this clearly yet. Our eyes are still darkened, 'tis said. But myself, I have become remarkably bright-eyed these last few cycles. And today, by a sudden mutational jump, I have developed jewel eyes which bring in unbelievable light to me. The fragments of me cannot communicate with one another on a conscious level. And yet we do communicate, for we are the architects of our own personality. It is possible that you and the other members of my inner cult may recognize my replacement, the alternate me, when he comes. If not, someday some others will recognize another parallel. Nothing of me will ever be lost. I leave it to you. If he seems to be a false replacement, or too slight an arrival, then you will dispose of him. It will be me whom you are killing, of course, but I can stand a lot of killing. The winnowing out of my lesser selves is not displeasing to me. There is no way at all— Well, there *is* one all-but-impossible way, but we'll not consider it. There is no way that all of me can be trapped and destroyed in one body. Ah, Fairfronter, you may want to polish up some of these sayings a little and incorporate them into my cult."

"I will, sir, I will. But the sayings will not be like yourself. Are there any arrangements that you want us to make for tonight, Mr. Dusmano? Have you decided how it is that you want to die?"

"Ah, there are at least two good possibilities of my being murdered. I always like that, if I have time to get into the right state of mind for it. I don't like to be caught unawares by my own murder. When I have my mind controlled, I can turn the power of the assault to my own advantage. No, the only arrangements that you people can make are to stand by and await possible orders. I am very flexible on these things. Oh, Fairfronter, the assailants are always so tense. Have you noticed that? I will see you later in the day or the evening, then, Fairfronter."

"Yes, and do be careful, Mr. Dusmano. You are the only cult figure for us. I really wish you weren't." Fairfronter left the company of Dusmano and talked to other persons in the Media Club.

Pilgrim Dusmano ate meerschaum cheese, which is made from cetacean milk. He ate it with one of those special small-cupped long-handled spoons with which informal diners have always eaten meerschaum cheese.

Another young Lord Spiritual came and sat at table with Pilgrim. But there was something very tricky about this young Lord. He was from the Provinces, and very little was known about him. But contrary things about him quickly became evident. The young Lord had a furtive look, and a real Lord will never, anywhere, have a furtive look.

The young man had the heart of a spy. For several hours Pilgrim Dusmano, with his mutated jewel eyes, had been able to see within people. The young Lord had the heart of a spy, and it beat fearfully through his bosom. Worse, it was the heart of a squeamish spy, a weak heart, a flutter heart in a flutter person. This man was no real Lord Spiritual. Oh, he would have his credentials in order, but he could never be lordly in his viscera. He was named Trenchant, and the more genuine of the younger Lords Spiritual had taken to calling him "the Rubber Knife."

"Mr. Dusmano," this mock Lord now said nervously (the false Lord had been speaking for some time, but to no particular moment), "you are a great man and I am abashed to challenge you. Yet I am obliged to question you, even though all the others here accept you without question. Is it possible that you are in the middle of making a great mistake?"

"No. I make many mistakes, young camel, but always on the side of temperance," Dusmano said. "I made the mistake of acquiring only one million dollars today instead of two million. I made the mistake of rearranging only twenty young minds instead of forty. I made the mistake of raping only one young man and one young woman today instead of half a dozen of each. There are days when the energy runs low, and the fullest pleasure seems rather in doing less than doing more. Yes, this is a mistake, but it isn't a great one. I have killed only one man today. That's a mistake, for the day is already half done. I can't count messengers as killed persons, for with them the killing is only a technicality."

"You will have killed nine by tonight if you aren't stopped," the mock Lord said. "Don't you know that in hounding down the Consul and others, you are knocking out some of the props that support the world? What if the human world itself collapses?"

"Oh, if this and other worlds collapse, perhaps we will enter the postworld era. Worlds are arbitrary divisions anyhow, and we could surely find some better grouping or arrangement of things. I question whether worlds are authentic categories or if they matter."

"Well, I am going to try to stop you in your destructions, Mr. Dusmano."

"How stop me?" Dusmano sneered. "Why would anyone want to stop me? I am an elemental force. As well want to stop the wind or the sun. But I will not be able to count all these kills as mine. We athletes of the kinkier pleasures do not count our assists as full kills. I do intend to have another full kill very quickly though."

"Evenhand is such a good man," the young mock Lord said. "Even the Forum Lords, the Pressmen Lords, the Tinsel Lords, the Media Lords cannot find one bad thing against him. And they have been searching for several hours."

"Oh, young colt, we've found any number of things against him. Even for a Consul to be unmasked is for him to come under an evil omen," Dusmano said. "And should a man be counted good who is under a bad omen? In this, the postanarchic age, the *arkhē* or rule of any Consul or official is bad, and it is made bearable only by a mask. But when the mask falls, then we must deem him—"

"But it was *you* and yours who tore the mask off him! And after you have torn it off, you convict him of not having the mask on."

"Certainly, young goat. A lack of agility in a Consul or anybody is bad; and it shows a lack of agility to be trapped in something so simple. There are other things. On the day that Evenhand became Consul three years ago, there was an earthquake in the Western Sierras."

"The average is more than two such quakes a day in the Westerns."

"The average, yes. But there are days of no quakes at all. Would not fair fate have given a good man an unquaking day for his first one in office? And there are worms in the apples on the Oceanic Coast. Would this happen if a good man were in office?"

"These things are not guilts, Mr. Dusmano! They are not reasons; they are not failings!" the mock Lord cried vehemently. "They are gnats; they are mere gnats! They are the little gnats of the age of unreason."

"Would there be gnats in the time of a good Consul?" Dusmano asked, making that let-us-be-reasonable gesture with his flowing hands. "We must avoid, young calf, not only the reality of evil but also the merest whisper of it. You have heard of the Lords of the Gnats? Gnats, mock Lord, are the whispers of evil."

"But I've heard that you yourself are a member of the Lords of the Gnats."

"So I am. But I'm no whisper of evil. I'm a shouting of evil. Don't you know that all worlds and all words have been turned upside-down?"

"But how do you justify such madness, Mr. Dusmano? How do you justify this detailed straining at gnats, you and your sort, when you consider the great and ungainly camels that you have swallowed whole and passed through you and out again?" Trenchant the mock Lord was challenging. "Yes, you pass them through complete with hair and hump and hoofs, and never a difficulty at all."

"Cleansing for the tract, camels." Dusmano smiled. "Very."

"Here, sir, are the Lords Pressmen, the Lords Forum, the Lords Articum, the Lords Tinsel, yes, and the Gnat Lords. Here are all the Lords Spiritual and Lords Media who have declared permanent revolution against the people and their delegates!" the spy, the mock Lord named Trenchant, was calling out angrily. "I do not believe that such people as you should be called Lords Spiritual at all."

"Have a care, young hogget," Pilgrim warned. "You have tripped the alarm with your anticultic and antielectronic reasoning and vehemence. Now the young Lords gather like buzzards."

And some of the younger Lords Spiritual were gathering ominously against the mock Lord, Trenchant; against the excited spy. Trenchant was not a good spy. By his raising his voice and passion in the club of his enemies he forfeited the right to be considered competent in even this temporary craft.

"There was a man who served as Consul, without thanks and without pay, a totally good man," Trenchant, the mock Lord, was arguing blindly in a thick and heavy voice. "And this good man will be torn apart limb from limb if the temper of this day holds the way that you have planned it. Why, great man, why?"

"The people will develop a taste for the blood of totally good Consuls," Dusmano said. "We encourage them in 'freedom of taste.' And you do not?"

"Your machinations call to heaven for vengeance!" the mock Lord shrieked.

"They call. But who will answer?" Pilgrim Dusmano laughed.

"Mr. Dusmano, you are *not* the true Peter Pilgrim of myth!" the incompetent spy stormed. "You are another and falser Pilgrim. And your whole cult is false."

This struck Pilgrim. If he was not the Peter Pilgrim of myth, then who was he? He knew that in reason he could not be that Peter Pilgrim. But he knew that they lived in the postreason era. In clear and simple unreason he would still be Peter Pilgrim, that authentic person of himself. Was he not himself a Media Lord and an Eidolon Lord? Or was he himself a mere eidolon made by drunken Lords for their amusement?

Several hard-eyed young Media Lords came and seized the mock Lord. They half blew out his life candle with their first assault. They left one eye dangling on the mock Lord, a throat torn open, and the man bloodily unmanned. They'd have killed him in an instant. But—

Pilgrim Dusmano intervened.

"My kill," Pilgrim said sternly. The disregard of precedence and the lack of ritual had offended him. The young Lords fell back, properly abashed.

"How do you want to do it, sir?" they asked. They deferred to Pilgrim now, as a cult figure. "With knife, mace, or cleaver, sir?"

"With my hands," Pilgrim said. And Pilgrim was powerful with his hands. Never mind that a man code-named Mut had handled him like a child that morning. After this day, Mut would handle no other man like a child, ever. But Pilgrim handled the dangle-eyed spy, Trenchant, that false Lord Spiritual, as though he were a segmented worm. A fool should never be allowed to live; and this sniveler had been a fool to play a double game as Lord Spiritual.

Pilgrim tore loose the tendons and broke the bones of the man. Strong pleasure flowed in from the strong, killing hands. Pilgrim broke the body open as though it were a bloody box. He quickly had the heart and the great omentum out and in his hands. He had the flickering life in his fingers, and he extinguished it with his terrible grip. Swift, sure pleasure, vital and mortal, that! The beauty of unshaping a corpus and raveling the life and intricacy clear out of it! Quick joy, and quick final glutting on that joy. And Pilgrim was finished with his kill.

Others of the Lords then broke the body down further, and they passed pieces of it to many interested organizations that had representatives there. Then several of the young Lords gathered up what was left of the false Lord. They took the remaining pieces of him back to the kitchen and hung them on butchers' hooks.

Pilgrim, almost surfeited with such pleasure, went out to smoke and to drink interprandial rum on the veranda. There was surfeit of other things. There is always a certain ennui about the last day of one's life, after it has been decided that it will be the last day. And Pilgrim was waiting for the interruption that he knew would come.

Noah Zontik, who was both a Lord Temporal and a Lord Spiritual, who wore both the pin of the Golden Shovel and the small Pilgrim Staff of the Pilgrim Dusmano Cult, came and joined Pilgrim there. And Pilgrim quickly and quietly affixed an insignia to his own mantle when he heard Zontik approach. It was the Iris Umbrella of Zontik himself. It was the sign that Pilgrim was under the protection and advocacy of Noah Zontik as a client of his.

"You have been behaving reprehensibly today, Pilgrim," Noah said sternly. "And it *is* my business, since I hold contract to guard and protect you. Moreover, you are my friend from the very heart. I worry for you more than for any other client or friend I have. In addition to this, I share a madness with many others: I belong to the Pilgrim Dusmano Cult. Oh why, why? Why have I traded my reason for such a trivial madness? You are utterly wrong about almost everything, Pilgrim, and yet I find myself giving surety for you, even to God. I don't understand myself, and you are like to lose your life this night, Pilgrim, for your sinfulness."

"A life is always well lost, Noah, if it is for a really successful and fulfilling sinfulness. Do you not yet understand that sinfulness is the aim of life, the culmination? Without this aim and fulfillment, life would have no concord. But how am I likely to lose my life this night, Noah?"

Pilgrim was now eating bleu cheese and mistignette mushrooms on a sideboard there on the veranda. One of the young Media Lords came out to him and brought a token that had once been a pendant.

"Perhaps he had once worn it around his neck and under his shirt," the young Lord said. "But now he had it under the skin, under the skin of his neck. It was in the flesh of the neck of the spy, Mr. Dusmano, the spy that we called 'the Rubber Knife.' We almost didn't see it. It's yours, of course, since the spy was your kill."

"Thank you," Pilgrim said softly. The token was a leather and hair badge of a group known as "the Camel's Revenge."

"Ah, he was one of the order of the humpbacked flesh. Do you believe, Zontik, that those of the common and camelous clay could really be avenged on a fire-flesh person like myself?" Pilgrim asked lightly.

"Yes. I think they can, and I'd wish they would, if I weren't under this foolish compulsion to protect you. Yes, it is the Camels who will kill you tonight, Pilgrim, if you're not careful," Zontik warned. "Or it will be one of the other groups equally outraged by your behavior."

"I'll try to arrange that it be the Camels," Pilgrim said. "I'll guide the affair and I'll lead it. And I'll draw the Camels right into my trap."

"How? Into what trap, Pilgrim?"

"I'll trap them into killing me, Noah. Is that not clever of me? I always wanted to be done to death by mad Camels. You see, Noah, I'm leaving tonight."

"Leaving town, Pilgrim?"

"Leaving the world, Noah, and leaving life."

"Ah, it's more of your damned foolish talk, Pilgrim."

"I boast that I'm foolish and I hope that I'm damned. I've always believed that damnation was the ultimate pleasure but that it had been given a hard name so we would deny ourselves the experience. I believe there is an elite group that wishes to preserve damnation uncrowded for its own members. I may join them on my own terms. For you see, Noah,

I'm not quite as other men are. I will live all the lives of my own parallels, and I am regenerated by walking on new worlds. We talked of such things this morning, Noah, but you didn't quite understand."

"I understand that I'm assigned to guard and protect you, Pilgrim. I can't recall who it was who assigned me to that not very pleasant task, but I believe it was done before the world began."

"Before *which* world began, Noah? But are you not also assigned to protect Evenhand, he who is now unmasked and revealed as the precarious Consul? Isn't he another of your clients?"

"He is my client and my friend, as you are. I am responsible for him. It is both for him and for you that I'm here. I intend to save both lives and souls of the two of you, though you seem not to want to be saved. That is no matter. I am a good protection man, and I will protect both of you, my clients."

"Both blades won't cut, Noah. Evenhand is my one powerful enemy on this world, just as you are my one powerful friend. I doubt if Evenhand is up to hating me even now. He didn't choose me as enemy, I chose him; he's perfect at the role. I must effect it that you do not succeed in protecting him, or me. Both Evenhand and I leave this world tonight. We have an appointment against each other at a tricky place over the edge, but he doesn't know of that yet."

"If both of you go from this world, then I go too," Zontik mumbled. "I have not been told that I'm restricted to this world. I've but been told to do my jobs. But you are prodigal of your own lives, Dusmano. You play a game that others are afraid to play because you believe that you have lives aplenty. But no man has an infinite number of lives. Not even you. Not even if you can do what you believe you can do."

"Yes, I'll have billions of lives, Noah, but not an infinite number of them. It doesn't pinch me as much yet as it will in a hundred billion years, after the odds have tightened on me a little."

"One of the lives will have to be on Prime World, Pilgrim."

"That also I will begin to worry about in a hundred billion years. Will you come inside and eat the final course with me?"

"I will not. I believe that you eat abominations today."

And pleasurable abominations they were that Pilgrim ate. He went to table inside the Club again. One plate only was set before him. One short shisk-spear was beside it, the only table utensil. One great glob of roasted flesh-meat was on the plate. There was no condiment. This flesh-meat was its own condiment. There was no bread, no wine. The meat was its own everything. The chef stood there in quiet triumph.

"It's Blut." The chef spoke in intense transport.

"Of course," Pilgrim whispered in his intricate voice. He stabbed the rich red ritual roast meat with the shisk-spear, and he began to eat. He had a godly gleam in his eye such as cult figures often have. But his was a new and mutated gleam.

"The burned flesh is pleasant in my mouth," Pilgrim said.

There are pleasures that less favored persons hardly know about.

7

For he who lives more lives than one
More deaths than one must die.

O. Wilde

And when the ritual hounds are done
The dead are you and I.

Hound Dog Huckster

Pilgrim Dusmano engaged a knacker of a special sort that afternoon. This knacker did not deal much in the bodies of dead animals. He did not pick them up from the streets and roads and pastures and haul them to the soap and oil extractors and to the processors of dog meat and cat meat.

Sometimes he did deal with the bodies of dead men, but more often he dealt with the fortunes and commerces and affairs that were left derelict by the deaths of those bodies. Sometimes a quick and knowing knacker can board a hulk-ship of fortune or affairs and declare it derelict when it wasn't quite so before. And by declaring it so, he can sometimes make it to be so.

It's a fine question whether a knacker can be counted as a Lord Spiritual, though often in his business he runs athwart spirits departing, and spirits refusing to depart.

Pilgrim Dusmano had engaged this talented knacker to arrange to pick up the affair-bones and to scrape the fortune-marrow of nine men. These nine men were the Consul Evenhand and his associates, with the code names of Blut, Brut, Flut, Glut, Gut, Hut, Mut, and Wut. All of these men had been propertied and rich beyond the needs for dishonesty. All were a little bit unguarded in their wealth in the manner that only a few very high men, mistakenly secure in their innocence, will carelessly allow to happen. And all these nine men were newly dead today, or they would be dead by the fall of night.

To swoop it all in! That would be the last great commercial stroke for Pilgrim Dusmano before leaving the world. This would be the real final pleasure, a break-bone and blood-suck pleasure. The red joy of it, gathering in all the fine property with its long roots with bits of flesh still clinging to them, would go far to nourish even the parallel Dusmanos on alternate worlds or aspects. It was a corporate good, really.

These dead or soon-to-be-dead men had all been declared traitors to the commonweal, and their property had been denominated derelict. In such cases, a trustworthy and knowing man can be declared governor or guardian over the property. And where was there a more trustworthy or knowing man than Pilgrim Dusmano?

Part of this property was of a sort that Pilgrim, but fewer than ten other men in the whole world, really knew something about. For a substantial part of it was property that was not even visible on this world.

There was, for instance, off-the-world commerce, particularly in the affairs of Evenhand. Evenhand had not conducted his off-the-world commerce by the same methods as Pilgrim had conducted his own. Evenhand had operated by "blissful permit," for he was a saint. Evenhand had not been fully conscious of his distant commerce, any more than Pilgrim Dusmano had been completely conscious of his own. Pilgrim had already ascertained that he could not operate by "blissful permit" between any two worlds at all. Nor could he use Evenhand's "blissful permit" even though he burdened himself with Evenhand's property and processes. There are rules out on the interworld routes. There are even monitors— not human monitors—assigned to enforce those rules. But the consolidation of Evenhand's commerce with his own would still profit Pilgrim in this world and the next, and the next, and the next.

Much of the knacker business of harvesting fortunes was conducted in that armored and secluded All-Effects Hall that was behind the Golden Grotto of the Pilgrim Cult. Mary Morey and her brother James were there, as they gave many hours to the grotto effects and knew most of the secrets. They were in charge of the furnaces where the golden images were cast. They were in charge of most of the machines.

"It helps that you are a certified cult figure," the knacker told Pilgrim Dusmano. "Cults are very strong this decade. Interworld they are absolutely blue chip. It hurts, though, that you do not come up to the moral minimum expected of cult figures, but that can't be helped. What we may give away in sanction, we may gain with power and speed. The combining of cults is always easier than one might believe. One flings documentary sleep broadcast into the eyes of all who oversee these things, and the eyes fall shut in most of the cases. I am drawing up certain documents and prophecies now that will add the Mut (Satterfield) Strength-in-Purity, Strength-in-Serenity cult to yours."

"Fine, knacker, fine." Pilgrim rubbed his charismatic hands

in pleasure and fulfillment. "Really, I believe I'm a better 'body beautiful' object than Mut is. He's a bit too knobby, a little too bulky. I must confess that he handled me like a child this day, but I'll handle him like a gooney in arranging his death. We may keep him here. We'll not have him torn to pieces like the others. We'll eviscerate him, fill his cavities with molten gold, and then we'll plate him with gold in one quick dip into the vat. Oh, he'll make a fine cult statue! And then we may add another cult statue today. This is the day for growing and addition. I'll not leave a mean grotto for the bright-eyed charismatic parallel myself who will come when I go. I always like to do well for myself and to give myself a good welcome when I come to a new place."

"Which would the other cult statue be, Dusmano?" the knacker asked. "I can think of none but Mut who would fit in here."

"Never mind the other. So far he's only a sudden idea that has come into my mind. And yet I believe he will fit in well. And as to Mut—well, I have these two young gold workers here, and there's a lot of ingot gold and statued gold to be derived from the Mut Cult."

"Yes, there is, Dusmano, quite a lot. And I will take my own share, my own pay, out of the Mut gold. One of the loves of my life is fancy and enabling paper, but in the final call I prefer present gold to any written title for it. I will have it today, Dusmano, today, in heavy ingot gold and in artful statue gold."

"Tomorrow," said pilgrim.

"Today," the knacker insisted. "I'm knacker enough to know which body will not be alive tomorrow."

"I *will* be here tomorrow, knacker," Pilgrim gave gestured assurance. "I become aware of a certain synchronicity in all this. I will leave, and at no great distance I will arrive soon after. Yes, I will be here tomorrow. I myself, though I may appear a little bit changed."

"You will appear so changed that you will not remember me or our bargains," the knacker accused. "You will be so changed tomorrow that you cannot be tied to pledges that you make today. You will be so changed that you cannot be positively identified as yourself. I want the Mut gold here now, within the hour. Send these two young people to bring it in that big dray there. It is a very sturdy dray. It will carry, I believe, the gold tonnage that I require, the tonnage which I calculate should be found at the Mut Cult."

"We haven't set up the apparatus to grab it yet, knacker," Dusmano said. "Cult transfers are intricate even when the power is in one's favor. But I assure you that I will set up the transfer procedure a little later in the day."

"I am setting up the transfer procedure now, Dusmano," the knacker said. "It's late enough in the day. I have drawn up authority of guardianship for these two young people. They will become convincing guardians of the Mut Cult gold, and they will bring it here. I have the documents ready now, though you would not recognize some of them as documents. These two will bring the gold here with no great trouble."

"And how much of it are you demanding?" Pilgrim asked.

"Never mind. Have them bring it *all* here, Dusmano. How can we count it when it is partly here and partly there? Bring it here, and then we will cast portions. These young people will pass for the roles, yes, with a bit more documentation. You know that my documentations sometimes go beyond the conventional. Now I will give a numinous quality to these two. It will stagger their brains, but it will not otherwise hurt them. 'Twill give them a glowing beauty, in fact. See! That's an effect they and you should learn in this House of Effects. They are lighted up with the auferous glow itself, are they not?"

Mary and James Morey did indeed light up with golden

shine. They seemed to be transcendent people, cloud-walkers. There was a divinity glow on them.

"This simple trick has been known for millennia," the knacker informed them, "but it has never been known by more than three men in this world at any one time. And one of those men, for all those millennia, has always been an ancestor of mine."

These knackers and their despicable trade, they have never been highly regarded by people. But animals have respected them for attending to their remains, and animals recognize fitness in this field. The remains that the knacker was attending to now were not quite animal, though they'd have become smelly residuals without this expert care.

"Be careful that you two don't harm or break anything," the knacker told the two Moreys. "Numinosity is always accompanied by exceptional strength."

"I know, I can feel it," Mary said. "And I like mine," she added, referring to her numinous glow. "But they *know* us at the Mut Body Cult temple. We cult people visit and talk shop. They know us as belonging to the Pilgrim Cult. They won't turn over any boodle to us. They won't believe that we are prophesied guardians."

"I said that my documentation went beyond the conventional," the knacker insisted. "So I will document the faces of the two of you to a new appearance. I have the information and templates on two honored and dead and departed members of the Mut Cult. They are such persons as will be accepted as returning from the grave. See, it's done. You two now look exactly like those two honored and dead cultists. And you also look just as the Mut Cult people would expect prophetic guardians to look. The Mut Cult people aren't overly astute. Frankly, they're not much smarter than the Pilgrim Cult people. What? Have I said something wrong? Forgive me. I'm only a poor blunt man and a knacker. I haven't the niceties. But I do have my talents. Go now, you two."

"Yes, go and get it, Mary and James," Pilgrim Dusmano gave the soft order. "Do it all very quickly. Even the mist in the eyes raised by a good knacker will not last forever."

"Prophetic or not, look-alike with a dead girl or not, I don't like my new face," Mary protested. "Will it wash off, or what?"

"It will wash off about as well as any other hypnotic projection will wash off, girl," the knacker said. "It will wear off, as all immaterial projections and documents do. Hurry, so it does not wear off before you two are finished."

Mary and James Morey took the large powered dray and went out from the All-Effects Hall that is behind the Golden Grotto. They went to pick up cult gold and other cult power and property.

And the knacker continued to forge enabling documents. But forge is not quite the word for what he was doing. As a younger man, the knacker had falsified instruments and forged supporting documents for them. But when a thing grows large and respected, then the small words will no longer serve. There should be better words than "forge" and "falsify" to describe the things the master knacker was doing.

In his earlier days the knacker had documented animal bodies with skinning knife or bone saw, or he had documented them with his haul-away wagon. Now he documented and processed larger and smellier bodies with more varied instruments. It was for some of the great and unhandy disposals he had made that he had been created a Lord Spiritual. This knacker was one of the uniquely capable men in that postanarchic world.

These were big carcasses, the mortal remains and residues of nine men: the Consul Evenhand, who was Rut, and his eight associates, Blut, Brut, Flut, Glut, Gut, Hut, Mut, and Wut. These wealths, these fortunes, these commerces, these accumulations were the bodies, just as well as the flesh-meats were the bodies. Pilgrim was not the only great man who lusted for these accumulations. He may have been the only one who lusted so strongly for the flesh-meat bodies and slaked his lust on them. But there were other money giants who longed to become more giantlike on this prey. The usual way was to divide such wealths with gauged snarlings and bluffings. But Pilgrim had rashly put out the word that he was claiming everything. "These are my kills," he said, posting his property claims.

And how long could he bluff the other powerful ones away from his kills? They would fang their way in tomorrow sure and overwhelm the foolish Pilgrim who had overplayed his hand and left himself vulnerable.

But Pilgrim was leaving this life and this world tonight, and he had not overplayed his hand for the short time that he had left. He would leave a death's-hand on his fortunes, and a death's-hand is often harder to remove than a living hand. And tomorrow there would be in the arena an alternate, a parallel, a newly arrived Pilgrim who would have all the Pilgrim brains and daring, and a certain transworld impetus besides. He'd have the advantage that spook-arrivals from other worlds often have.

"We are always on our own in things like this," Pilgrim told himself and his sensing parallels. "We will do our corporate best, and we will bring many persons of us to bear at one point wherever the going is tricky. We get better at this all the time."

And Pilgrim and the knacker worked rapidly and with intuitive illogic. They printed, they planted, they cut and trimmed, they instigated, they pulled canny strings on deadfall traps. And they documented. Then, in a quick hour, Mary Morey and her brother James were back to the All-Effects Hall with the laden and groaning dray.

It was the biggest load of gold in the world, but it came

humbly dressed in sackcloth and ashes. Some of the rough sacks were bursting open from the weight of their metal, and the gleam shone through the ashes and trash that are commonly used to cover gold shipments.

Even Pilgrim was impressed. Even the knacker was. One does not come on fortunes like Mut's (Strength-in-Purity Cult, Strength-in-Serenity Cult) every day.

"I've no greed in me at all," the knacker said. "You take eight parts, and I take one. You take all the loot of the other eight men, including the empires of that good man Evenhand. And I will take all the gold of Mut that these young persons have brought. What does it weigh?"

"A bit over twenty-six thousand kilograms," James Morey said.

"Thank you, good young people. Thank you, good strong dray," the knacker said. "Now we will take this gold quickly to—"

"We will take it nowhere till you have finished your job, knacker," Pilgrim Dusmano said. "You have not yet knackered the material remains of Wut, who is rage or mania. Wut is very, very rich. I want that rageful property processed at once. Then we will see about dividing the gold of the Mut Cult which gleams here so beautifully."

"There'll be no dividing the Mut gold," the knacker warned. "It's all mine." And he was weighing the three of them with his eyes. He would draw this out a bit. There was a leftover situation here that would go away in a few moments.

"I never finish a job till I have been paid in full. Dusmano, we've completed the processing documents for eight men and eight fortunes. And you are impatient for the ninth? No, we will hold rich Wut over. Let me have all this Mut gold stowed safely in a place of my own; let me have it received and garrisoned by my own people. Then we will come back here and process the fortune of Wut. Really, his should be slightly greater than that of Mut, though not in so delightful a form."

"Mary!" Pilgrim Dusmano called sharply. "Quickly, quickly!"

Pilgrim also understood about the leftover situation here that would go away in a few moments. Mary and James still had their numinous strength, till it should falter. Mary pinioned the knacker. Then she began to mutilate him with a knife. Had he needed to document so strong a numinosity in these two young people?

"James, quickly, quickly!" Pilgrim called, and James began to shovel and throw gold into the furnace that Pilgrim had already fired.

"You told me to be careful that I did not harm or break anything, did you not, knacker?" Mary laughed as she opened the belly of the knacker without harming or breaking anything much. She worked with almost surgical precision. "And you said that numinosity was always accompanied by exceptional strength. Oh, it is, and I'm in love with it. Pardon if I hurry, knacker-man, but we all know that my strength is for only a little while."

It became more difficult then. Mary was emptying the visceral cavity of the knacker-man, and this cannot be done without harm or breaking. Her numinous godly strength had ebbed, but that of the mutilated knacker-man was gone completely.

"You break thieves' honor, Dusmano," the knacker gasped in his torture.

"I know, I know," Pilgrim gloated. "How slow thieves are at understanding that in the postanarchic world thieves' honor has become a patchy thing! But I build my own honor so high that no one can see just how broken it is."

"You throw away the Wut fortune for the glittering Mut hoard, which is less," the knacker grunted slowly and painfully. "And you make a strong and dangerous enemy—me."

"Dying enemy, how will you touch me? But maybe I do not throw away the Wut fortune," Pilgrim said. "I am no mean knacker myself, and I have just been watching the best knacker in the world at his documentation. I'll try it myself on the Wut holdings. And I worry not at all that a dying dog should hate me."

"I'm onto as many tricks as you are, Dusmano," the knacker gave out in agonizing gulps. "I also am leaving this world today by your decision. But you thought I knew not what to do nor how to handle it. These things I do know. For your intemperance, I leave the world now, several hours before you do. I'll prepare a welcome for you in a new place, man. Oh, how I'll prepare a welcome for you!"

"You'll go to no new place, knacker," Pilgrim said. "You don't know how."

"If you'd touched me yourself in any of this murder, I'd have had you spooked, Dusmano," the failing knacker moaned.

"Yes, I know," Pilgrim said placidly. "I know about the bad-death touch of the knackers. Several times you thought to lunge to touch me. You couldn't have done it."

Mary Morey was now having more trouble with the limp knacker. The exceptional strength that always accompanies numinosity had faded clear away, now that the numinosity was gone. It didn't matter, except that the going was slower. The strong knacker was dying, and now he was far beyond resistance or words. The molten gold was ready to be poured from the flash-furnace.

"We will want a better expression than that for a cult figure, knacker," Pilgrim gibed at the eviscerated man. "We want the expression of one who is looking into the innermost depths of something. Please, please, we want an interesting expression. And yours is dull."

Mary Morey went out from the All-Effects Hall.

"His expression will change when hot gold is poured into his cavity," James Morey said. "But I don't know whether it will change for the better or for the worse. Even if he is dead, his expression will change in some gaping rictus."

"There isn't any better or worse that I know about," Pilgrim said. "There are no such opposites in the postanarchic world. I want something cultish to show on that face. Eight-ninths-dead knacker, you are trying my patience sorely."

"It is ready, Mr. Dusmano," James Morey said, wheeling the great, glowing bucket above the gape-belly knacker.

Mary Morey came back into the All-Effects Hall. She carried the dead body of a goat-kid. Never mind where she had gotten it in so short a time, it was a small and recently dead body.

"Dead-eyed knacker, look, look with your dead eyes!" she invited, and she put the small goat body before his ashen face and blank eyes. And at the same moment her brother James began to pour the melted gold into the body cavity of the knacker. Ah, a great pour! More than two hundred kilograms it was. The dying-dead body jerked, and a new expression came onto the death face.

"You wanted all the gold, knacker. Now have it. Have a belly full," Pilgrim said vulgarly.

The expression on the new cult face that had belonged to the knacker was one that few people would understand. But animals, who have respected knackers for attending to their remains, just might have understood something of it. The face was a gaping rictus, yes, and it was so red that it was black. But in its death agony the face now showed the strangest compassion ever. Someone, something might understand it. The small goat body probably understood it. Even the people of the cult might understand it someday. Cult people often understand much more than do their cult figures. There was a unique expression on this new cult face.

It was the expression of one who was looking into the innermost depths of something.

All the light and numinosity had gone out of Mary Morey then. She was once again a freckled, rusty-haired, unlarge girl who was in the middle of a tangled and worried adolescence. It's worse when one is entangled with a cult figure. She sat in the bright light of the All-Effects Hall and gave herself over to dirty-faced weeping.

The glowing bucket had done its work and was withdrawn. James Morey now maneuvered the lifting fingers of a big hoist under the body of the knacker. He lifted the body easily, with only a feather touch on the controls. Easy, easy, so that the body wouldn't tear completely apart with its load of not yet solidified gold.

And then the dipping of that body into the vat of the flash-furnace itself. Oh, it would be beautifully coated and plated there! It would come out of there as an authentic cult image, golden and startling. Give it a minute, give it five, measured only by the sniffling of Mary Morey.

And then the new statue was hoisted out, dripping with the rippling fire of molten gold, ponderous and powerful, breath-catching with the pain and compassion of that slaughtering and knacking man who had died on a croaking catch of a last breath, and who had reacted after he was dead to the need of a goat-kid asking care and disposal.

Mary Morey understood then, and gave the kid body that care and disposal.

The gilded knacker hung there in the skylike height of the All-Effects Hall, pulsing with its own golden incandescence. The ponderous doorways between the All-Effects Hall and the Golden Grotto were thrown open, and the new cult statue was rolled out into the Grotto. Workmen were just completing a pedestal there.

"Make another one," Pilgrim Dusmano ordered. "We

pre-empt this one." The knacker-statue was set slowly onto the pedestal.

"There's a glow to it beyond the glow of gold," James Morey said with a touch of fear. "I've never seen a thing like it."

"I have," Pilgrim said. "You dipped it so well and so cannily, boy, that the soul had no chance to escape. It's trapped inside, forever."

There was a sigh from the statue. There was contradiction in the sound of it. Cooling but still incandescently hot gold will sometimes sigh almost like that. Almost like. So will a soul, making a tricky escape, sound like that.

"It needs a name!" Pilgrim called out, and raised his hands. It was as though he were commanding that a name should descend on the statue. "We must invent a name for it, a name that our cult people will spontaneously apply to it when they first view it."

"The name of it is 'the Holy Knacker,' " Mary said. And that is the name of it to this day.

James Morey stood in the shadows, out of the bright light of the All-Effects Hall, out of the cascading brilliance of the Golden Grotto. More and more often he stood in shadows these days. The gold lust and the blood lust had drained out of him, as it would never drain out of Pilgrim Dusmano. James was sobbing silently, but maybe not tearlessly.

It's a hard thing for young persons to be attached, body and soul, to a cult figure. It's as though they became mere eidolons of an eidolon, mere graven images of a graven image.

To save a self, perdition bent,
What does a ten-thumbed, murksome
  meddler?
Which plea to God should he present,
The unctuous umber-ella peddler?

Golden Grimoire

"Pilgrim Dusmano is such a good man," Mary Morey said, "that I would change every name on everything else in the world rather than say that he was anything else. I will say that white is black, I will say that sweet is sour, I will say that up is down (and I'm not sure that it isn't), and I will say that Pilgrim is a good man. What we need to do is convince the Lord of the Worlds of this fact. But how will estranged ones like ourselves even get an audience with him?"

There were eleven of them sitting there in the sunlight of what Rhinestone Suderman said was "the last sunny day ever in this world for us." These persons sitting in the sunlight were Mary Morey, Rhinestone Suderman and Howard Praise, who were students of Pilgrim Dusmano, as well as being disciples, catamounts, doxies, shills, and members of his cult. They were Clarence Music, who was curator of the Daylight Museum; Randal Muckman, who was a Media Lord; Judas Raffels and John Augustine, who were Doctors Medical; Spurgeon, who worked for Pilgrim in his commerces; Cord-cutter and Fairfronter, who had many points of contact with Pilgrim Dusmano; and Noah Zontik, the umbrella man.

There were eleven persons sitting in the sunlight, and one person, James Morey, sitting in the shadows. All of them were members of the Pilgrim Cult on some level.

"Pilgrim is not merely the projection of one particularly dull person, as someone, probably myself, has said," Noah Zontik was explaining. "He is the projection of several hundred very bright persons. And ultimately, as he becomes a living legend and his cult takes hold throughout the worlds and sends its eddies out and out, he will become the projection of millions of persons of all sorts.

"And we project what we want to be. Apparently we want to be crawling evil things, for Pilgrim is such, even where white is black and up is down. Why are *we* like that? I don't know. We aren't bad individually, except where we touch him. But the cult is evil, and that evil is generated either in ourselves or in Pilgrim. Does a transmission belt become evil as it transmits, or is the evil to be found in the power source? Or is it to be found at the point of power reception? Is Pilgrim more than a receptor of power? Is there anything real about him? If there were, it would be very difficult to find it. But the transmission belt is transmitting apace. All of the projections are of some effect. Pilgrim *does* change and develop as he becomes more and more a center of interest. There are aspects of him that he is not at all aware of. And his unconscious has its fragmented existence in thousands of

minds besides his own. He believes that these fragmented
containers are parallel beings of himself. I believe they are
ourselves, all who have ever taken part in his cults or
incorporations, here or elsewhere. And I am a man who does
not believe in an elsewhere, does not accept the multiplicity
of worlds either parallel to our own or scattered afar.
Nevertheless, if Pilgrim leaves this world and life tonight, I
will leave also. I don't believe in him, but I believe even less
in myself without him. And I have a commission from
beyond to guard him forever, and to share his destruction if I
cannot avert it. I believe that I have this commission from
beyond, but I do not believe in any beyond."

"And tonight he is leaving this world and we will not see
him again," Rhinestone Suderman mourned. "He has lighted
a light in each of us—what matter if it gutters and burns with
an uneasy and unorthodox reek? Will he remember or will he
forget to blow out those lights again before he leaves? And
what sort of things will we be without him, left to ourselves
with our unpleasant and stenchy burning?" Rhinestone was a
large young fair-haired female person.

"He *says* that we will see him again," Howard Praise
reminded them. "He says that a parallel aspect of himself will
come to us in his place."

"What is he, a Christus, that he should send us a Paraclete?" Fairfronter asked with false disdain.

"Yes, he says he is exactly that." Mary spoke like leaves.
She sat freckled and unaccountably brilliant in the sunlight.
Dappled and sun-beamed, she was daylight itself, freckled
daylight with clouds roiling up behind her.

"And he *is,* to us," James Morey said out of the shadow.

"Can we talk the end of the world away?" Howard Praise
asked worriedly. "Can we not act? Or has our activation been
transferred entirely to Pilgrim? Has he no care that he breaks
worlds like eggs when he passes through them? Will this

broken world be no more than a mirrored image of broken us and broken Pilgrim?"

The bawling and roaring and gibing of crowds of people could already be heard in the middle distance, and the daylight was not nearly spent.

"I believe that ours is a peculiar world and that we are a peculiar people," Noah Zontik said. "I doubt that most worlds are in the postanarchic era. I doubt whether many of them have even entered the period of full anarchy. The younger of you will not remember this, but here we had rejected all rule so completely that even now, in the post age, we will have no ruler unless he is anonymous and masked. And we will defame him at the least glance behind that mask. All we have to do is discover a human person behind that ruler and we will attack him to death. We will defame him and assault him to death if the Media Lords have their way about it. The Media Lords? They also are projections of ourselves. We have a lot of projections. We would have to be quite sick to have so many. We all have this blood lust for the murder of a ruler, but it cannot be a good thing, and ours cannot be a good age. But there is no one anywhere who has this blood lust as strongly as Pilgrim Dusmano has it, and he cannot be a good man. But if he is not good, then what are we? We make him a cult figure and a godlet. Well, perhaps he is the correct godlet for the postanarchic age."

"Have we not realized that Pilgrim himself is set up as a ruler, and that we ourselves are set up as his mask?" the Doctor Medical Judas Raffels asked. "But they'll not trap him as he trapped Evenhand, as others have been trapped. They will shatter the mask (ourselves), and there will be no Consul revealed behind it. Pilgrim will have gone, the pieces of him scattered throughout a thousand worlds and a million minds, and there will be nothing left."

"Oh, he never did have a face," the other Doctor Medical

John Augustine said. "He always had to have a mask, even before he used the corporate one that is the cult. I seem to remember him, somewhere, possibly not here, as living in body after body, speaking out of them, slaying them when they proved bad cover, going on to others and bursting or slaying them in turn. Before he was a world-jumper he was a body-jumper."

"That is your own personal projection of what he was and did, Doctor," Fairfronter cautioned. "It is only a slight bit of the total projection that is Pilgrim. It is only one of many slivers of his past, but I suppose it is authentic."

"Why are you two Doctors Medical here?" Clarence Music from the Daylight Museum asked. "What is there in him that attracts you? You are the two members of our cult who most bother me. The rest of us seem to be a part of his troubled and shattered spirit, his nonessentiality. But you two seem to be otherwise."

"His spirit? I don't believe in any spirit," the Doctor Medical Judas Raffels said. "My own interest is in his body, in his medical body. This is as much a mask thing as is his figurative face. Have you not noticed that he sometimes looks larger, sometimes smaller? That he is sometimes robust and sometimes extenuated? Have you not noticed that he is sometimes in the lower end of the spectrum and sometimes in the upper end? Surely you have noticed that his shadow refuses to follow his body."

"Oh, that's the case of all of us now," Mary said. "There was never any reason for shadows to be so fixed as they were in the past."

"Who notices your shadow?" Raffels asked. "Have you not noticed that Pilgrim Dusmano intercepts neither light nor heat nor wind? 'Twould do no good to choose the lee side of him."

"No. In many ways that does no good," James Morey said. "Have you not noticed that he seems weightless sometimes, and of an awkward pseudoweight at others? And he refuses to be touched and tested. He'll not be weighed in life; but I believe that once somewhere we did weigh him in death."

"He is inextricably allied with the Lords of the Media," Noah Zontik said sadly. "Shall I blame his evil on them? I must blame it on someone, since I am charged with delivering him from all evil. In no such time but this, on no other world but this, could the Lords of the Media have become so powerful. They serve no purpose. They attack purpose. They have no rightful authority. The thing they hate most is authority. I don't believe they would ever accept it, even for themselves—not without changing the name of it. But for the last century we've had no elected officials at all on our world. Yet the Media Lords, the most powerful of all the Lords Spiritual, do rule by election in its deeper sense. We have chosen them and we have elected them, but not by ordered voting. For there is no ordered rule on our world, no rationality. We have the calculated opposites of these things. For just as the Media represent the anti-intellect, just as the dissemination of the Media is the anti-illumination, so are the Media Lords the true Lords of Unreason and Darkness.

"Who brought it about?

"Someone must have thought of all this when he put tongues in human heads to talk with, when he put fingers on hands to signal with, when he put styli in fingers to write with, when he created the ethereal tinsel to carry waves of a hundred sorts to a dozen senses to communicate with, when he put ears and eyes in heads to receive with, when he put the perverse lobe in our brains to defame and subvert with. The Lord of the Worlds has put these things in these places. But shall we hold him, or ourselves, responsible?"

They walked down Sycamore Road, almost knee-deep in leaves. Vehicles were not allowed on Sycamore. It was rustic. People were dragging off old wood and cutting out sick and spindly bushes and trees. They would have bonfires and celebration fires tonight. People were sacking up leaves in huge plastic sacks to add to the pleasant reek of the evening fires.

"Do you know who it is who will kill Pilgrim in the end?" Fairfronter asked. "In the end, and this, of course, is the end. It will not be 'the Camel's Revenge' or any such societies that have stored up resentments against him. No, it will be the Media and the Lords of the Media with whom Pilgrim worked pestle in mortar for so long a time. The Media and their Lords rend and kill Consuls when they can find them behind their masks. And they kill them because of the good that is in them. And now they begin, as do all of us, to see behind Pilgrim's mask a little bit. And now they will kill him for—get this!—for the very small amount of good that is in him. What sophisticated microscopes they do have these days! Talk about straining at gnats! The microscopic good that is in Pilgrim Dusmano is the gnat reversed. Oh, how they are straining at it at this moment! Oh, how all the great Lords are straining at the stool! It's near to destroy them (the great camel-passers, they), as can be told by their groaning."

"All the final things are happening now," Doctor Judas Raffels said. "I seem to have a new sort of receiver, and I can tick them off in my head: anything that is happening anywhere in the city.

"Evenhand is dead and dismembered. Pilgrim has just dined on him, a rare, rich bit, and that in fine company. But something went weird there, weird even to the susceptibilities of Pilgrim; something turned weird in that fine company. There had not been such a fine dinner ever, perhaps. Nor so fine a company, not since the preanarchic days, at least. That full and rich dinner should have sated. It didn't. All the great men at that table looked around at one another."

"Since when have you had this little illuminated theater in your head?" Rhinestone asked him.

"Barely since the present moment," Raffels said. "The great men sat, and an idea formed about them on black wings. 'What next?' they asked each other with their nictitating snakes' eyes, or 'Who next?' 'What is the titillation beyond?' they asked. 'Somewhere there must be found either rarer food or ranker persons to devour it. And where are ranker persons than ourselves to be found?' Each man's eyes were on his neighbor.

"That was only a moment ago. Then the moment shifted. All the eyes of them were drawn to the nervous, magnetic fluctuations of the most attracting man present. Each man's eyes were on Pilgrim Dusmano, to destroy him and to devour him in fortune and flavor. And, finally, to devour ritual pieces of him literally.

"Even then, for a moment just now, it could have gone either way. It could be Pilgrim. Or it could be the rest of the Lords assembled. And Pilgrim was, or he had been, quite able to devour them all, almost, if the tide were running strongly enough in him, if he had full impetus and momentum.

"He has the extensible jaws of the python, you know: figurative jaws, figuratively extensible at least. He could have stretched those jaws over that whole company there, swallowing and smothering those Lords in a transparent and hardly visible membrane, doing them to death, and then eating them individually at his ecstatic leisure. Many men have lately been done to death by things absolutely transparent.

"Pilgrim Dusmano could have done this. Only he couldn't. And when the tide turned, it turned with a great slosh and splash. He tried to divert them with his mind and his voice and his flowing hands. They wouldn't be diverted. They would have no substitute. He swept for a moment very strongly against them and almost hurricaned them down. But his mind tires easily after a nervous day, and there were a number of strong minds against him. They beat him back.

Pilgrim bolted. He rushed out from that fine Club. Now he is a fugitive."

"Why should he be fugitive from anything?" Zontik asked. "He intended to trap the 'Camels' into murdering him tonight. What does it matter now if he is killed by the Lords instead?"

"He's lost his initiative," Raffels said. "His momentum is gone. Now he'll die afraid and beaten, and I've heard that it's the worst of luck to do that. They broke him! And that leaves him open to every danger and ambush on the road. I wish there were a way for me to withdraw from his cult."

"There isn't," said Doctor John Augustine. "That's as though one on a rational world should say, 'I wish I could unbelieve.' But nobody who has ever really believed can cease to believe. One may say that he has ceased. One may act as though he had. One may defame and defile and revile what one has believed in. But that one still believes, however blackly. And we will all still belong to this cult, however much the cult figure fails us. We'll prop him up with sticks and false witnesses. If the straw leaks out of him, we'll insist it is the ichor of the gods. We'll feed him with our own blood. But it'll be dark and chilly on our world after he's gone. He was our light and heat. It didn't matter that we first brought those things to him and laid them at his feet. It doesn't matter that he squandered and wasted them and was the least efficient cult figure ever. It seems yet—and we will erect it as an unquestioned fact—that all our light and heat come ultimately from this contemptible Pilgrim."

They all went to a small private upstairs room from which they could watch the bonfires and the murders when they began. Nobody knew who had arranged for them to come to this room, or to whom the room belonged. They should have been able to watch the fires and the deaths, except that there were no windows in the room.

"Why? Is there someone here, at this late time, who still

cannot see through walls?" Mary asked. "And if there is, why is he here?"

"There are a few clashes now," Doctor Raffels said while he rolled his eyes up and back as though reading an inward presentation. He was seeing things at various places in the city. "Certain militia of the Media Lords are battling with bravos of 'the Camel's Revenge.' It's all good clean battle, mostly for the forgotten joy of open fighting. It's one of the few clean things that are left these days. There's a clutch of dirty things gathering in the corners, though. It's been decided, not in these clashes and scuffles, but it's been decided that Pilgrim will go, and that he will go dirty."

"When became you a prophet or a seer over the distances?" Doctor John Augustine asked his colleague, Doctor Raffels. "I hadn't noticed that power in you before."

"Ah, John, we are all of us dripping with new powers. It's the season for it. Mine came quite recently, within the half hour, and with no warning at all that I would be cursed with such gifts. New talents always appear suddenly and completely. They'd be refused if they didn't set such quick roots into one before even the first protest could be made. And a rooted talent cannot be torn out, ever.

"Pilgrim is hiding now. He's in the largest thorn thicket along that parkway that he maintains. He's in good cover, and he'll not be found unless someone tells where he is."

"Why should Pilgrim hide?" Spurgeon asked. "He's always been fearless and serene, whether in his good or in his evil."

"Oh, he's an absolute coward!" Mary Morey contradicted in flashing anger. "He always has been. He's the tallest sniveler of them all. Why should anyone defend him? We all know he's worthless and that he makes us become worthless. But James and I will go with him whenever he goes. He'll need someone."

"And now the people are being carefully unconfused about things," Doctor Raffels said. "I don't trust the unconfusers, but they are illuminating things all over town, to everybody; and everybody had better listen, for the unconfusers are backed by force. It's being explained to the people which is their right hand and which is their left. The right and the left sometimes change places, and we will not even notice it unless we are dull as the common herd. That's why the right and the left must be explained in every changed time. The world flips over, and we find ourselves living on the reverse and unfinished side of it. The people are being told that Pilgrim Dusmano is deeply involved in the Evenhand affair. That's all that's needed to set them to howling. There are only two bloods left for the people to howl over now: the blood of Pilgrim Dusmano, and the blood of the man code-named Wut, he who's now in an innocent rage or mania."

"Pilgrim will be torn in the thorn thicket," Mary said. "We'd better go to him and give him heart for the end of it all. Even a coward can go grandly, if he is flowing-haired and of the dripping hands and elegant voice. Yes, and we'll give the people at least two more bloods to howl for and to drink. I don't want them to be thirsty."

"Pilgrim will be torn, but not in the thicket," Raffels said. "It's green-thorn time in the thicket. The bushes are just out of the bud."

"You're crazy," Fairfronter said. "This is autumn, and the thorns should be in full thorn."

"Maybe, but they're not. And Pilgrim will not be torn by the thorns. I see what I see. He has enough control over the times and the seasons to make it green-thorn time around him."

This had become a cult meeting in the small and unwindowed room. There was the particled walnut bread, the cult bread that Mary Morey took with tongs and placed on the tongues of the cult members. There was the grace cup, the parting cup that was filled with quince wine. But Doctor

Raffels did not wait for the ritual serving. He rudely put out his hand and seized the cult bread and ate it. He took the grace cup in his two hands and drank directly from it, disdaining to use the golden straw.

"So you are the one," Mary Morey said. "Who would have guessed that a great man and a doctor would be the one to break the cult?"

"Yes, I am the one who will break it," Raffels said, munching on the walnut bread and wiping his mouth. "Now I continue with my visions. Pilgrim Dusmano is doing some very nervous talking to himself. 'I will salvage what I can,' he is saying. 'It will be a bad jump, yes, but it need not be as bad for me as it would be for another. I have my powers and my balance. I can steer unwrecked past most of the shoals. I can catch fish in foamy waters. I'll have barratry profit even from my own shipwreck. Must I go at all? Likely I must. It is so hard to back out of a noose; it leaves the neck suspiciously marked forever. But I can jump, and jump, and jump again. I'll jump loose, and nobody will bind me. Who says one cannot mock death and transformation? One can mock anything if he's named Pilgrim Dusmano.' But that is only Pilgrim trying to brave-talk himself through a chancy evening. He's whistling down the dark caverns of his own mind, but he's scared clear out of that mind."

"Heavy footsteps," Howard Praise muttered. "They're not from the curly boots of the bravos. They're from the jackboots of the militia of the Media Lords."

"Even now at the door," Raffels mumbled. And there was a great hammering at the door.

"Open, open in the names of the Media Lords," came a clear and commanding voice.

"Name us some of their names," Mary jeered at the rattling door. "We're little people from the country and never heard of the Media Lords."

"This room and house are under the umbrella," Noah

Zontik called out. "They're under the protection of my own organization. They're certified and recognized and notarized as protected; they're recognized by the Media Lords and by others."

"We claim 'Freedom of Entry' under the authority of those same Media Lords," the clear voice called in. "In the world of Total Freedom, who can dispute our 'Freedom of Entry'?" The militiamen shattered the door and came in.

"Where is Pilgrim Dusmano?" the young man of the clear and commanding voice asked. "We have a warrant for his arrest."

"Let me see that warrant," Noah Zontik requested. "There's no reason for his arrest."

"Oh, it isn't a written warrant," the militiaman said. "It's a flesh-and-blood warrant. We have that warrant; we live that warrant, in every limb and line of us. Our own strength and the outreaching power of our Lords are our warrant to arrest any man. 'Freedom to Arrest' is one of the fundamental freedoms. Where is he? Shall we have twelve tongues out and floating in this bowl here, or will you tell us?"

"Nobody here will tell you," young Howard Praise said absolutely.

"Nobody, nobody, nobody," others of them said.

"Yes, there is one here who will tell," Mary Morey said. "It isn't I. It's another one."

"Dusmano is out by that parkway that is north of his commodity receiving area on the edge of town," Doctor Raffels said. "He is hiding in the largest thorn thicket there. Come. I'll show you."

The militiamen went out, and Doctor Raffels went with them. Raffels whistled a couple of bars of "Heads Will Roll" as he went. He didn't yet understand what sort of execution it would be.

Out on the edge of town, on that parkway of his, Pilgrim

Dusmano came out of a thorn thicket like a startled stoat at the approach of the militiamen. He was white-eyed and twitching with fear. The people gathered around him and howled for his blood. They began to buffet him. But a man who struck him found his hand withered, and the crowd fell back.

"Leave off the cheap tricks, Dusmano," a militiaman ordered sternly.

"Yes," Pilgrim said, "yes." He was whipped down to nothing.

And suddenly he surged up to everything again. He became the Pilgrim of old, the cult figure without equal. There was the curling and pleasant mockery on his mouth. There was the unbroken-horse look in his face, the look of the rebel forever. There was the incredible vulgarity in the set of his fat jaw. Pilgrim was again that handsome man with the contoured and flowing fair hair. He was the man with the powerful and carrying voice, the voice that was at the same time intricate and modulated, almost feminine. He was the man with the shimmer, with the dazzle about him. He was the hypnotic man, the electric man, the magnetic man, the transcendent man. He was the man with the flowing hands that dripped beneficence. He was the mythic man with the dripping hands.

But what does the term "dripping hands" mean, outside of its mysterious cult usage? His hands dripped light, they dripped dazzle, they dripped grace and gift. They dripped seed and solace. And the spreading-out of the hands was a grand gesture, whatever else it was.

Pilgrim Dusmano was not arrested by the militia of the Media Lords, not yet. It was rather that *he* arrested both the militia and the crowds. Pilgrim went, and everybody followed him. There was a persimmon tree beside the road. Pilgrim cursed it. "Its fruit is not of my cult," he said, and he went on.

Only Raffels and Zontik and Spurgeon and Mary and James Morey had followed the militiamen out from the cult meeting.

"Presumably we will look back and the tree will be withered," Noah Zontik said. "But I'll not look back."

"I will," Mary said. She looked back, and there was not any persimmon tree there, either withered or hale. "I don't believe there was ever any persimmon tree there, was there?" she asked.

"No," said Spurgeon. "I had to take an inventory of the trees in the region of the parkway. I took this once a month. There was never a persimmon tree there."

Pilgrim stood and talked with his hands spread out and his fair hair flowing. This was on a brown green knoll above the parkway.

"It will bloom again when I am gone," he said, "but not now. I've greened a dozen worlds with my leaving them. They green themselves in recollection of me. Listen now, and I'll give you the meat without the shell and the fruit without the rind.

"I preach you the declared thing with no opposite to restrict it. The high without the low, the light without the dark, the inside without the outside, the up without the down, the feast without the famine, the young and never the old, the beginning without the end, the circle without a center, the top without a bottom, the winning without the losing, the prize without the payment, the bait without the hook, the rain and never a drought, the exaltation and never a depression, the sin without the remorse, the right without the wrong, the shot without the recoil, the crime without the punishment, the inebriation without the aftermath."

"It doesn't mean a thing, does it?" Mary Morey asked.

"Why should it?" Zontik asked. "Do you look for meaning in a hymn?"

"It's a good trick," Doctor Augustine said to Doctor Raffels, "but can he deliver on it?"

"The trick is the nondelivery," Raffels said. "To deliver would be straight. John, I thought you were cowering with the others back in the cult room."

"A little cowering goes a long way with me. It's tedious. Raffels, I've been thinking that we might pick up some several stipends this evening. We are two very good medical doctors. Why should we let lesser doctors receive stipends for pronouncing persons dead, especially when they are rent apart and dead without any doubt? Both of us are Lords Spiritual, and we have rank to displace any lesser doctors looking for death-scraps."

"All right, John. We will do it. There's something familiar about this, however. I have the oddest feeling that I have attended Dusmano at his death at some earlier time."

"Possibly, possibly. Was I there?"

"Yes. I believe so."

"I proclaim the counterpart without the prime-part," Pilgrim was telling in his golden voice. "I speak of counter-worlds with no first world. I speak of counterculture, but there is no such thing as culture itself. I speak of derivatives, but there are no originals ever anywhere. I know antithesis, but not thesis. I love antilogy, but I blind my eyes to logy or logic itself. I recognize antimatter, but I have not seen matter. Look about you. Which of them do you see? Is it the thing, or is it the antithing?"

Then the voice of Pilgrim Dusmano became more drossy than golden.

"I myself am anticlimax. But who is climax? I am antihero. But there is no hero anywhere."

Pilgrim spread out his hands in a gesture that lacked a small something. Nowhere was there any gesture complete and unlacking. Antihero that he was, he stood like a Christus and spoke. Mary Morey understood that he was an Anti-Christus, but who else understood it? Then Pilgrim began to wilt as he saw horses being brought toward the knoll.

"I speak of attraction without distraction." Pilgrim was talking, but he was barely heard. His tongue was clay. He gulped as though he would try to swallow his last words. Now he hardly looked like an antihero even.

"It's just come into his mind that 'distract' originally meant to draw asunder or to tear to pieces," Raffels said to Augustine. "Now he sees the horse-beasts and he is in a clammy fear that his death will be a distracting by wild horses. The militia offers an interesting assortment of deaths, though. I wonder what mine will be?"

"Are you going with him, Raffels?"

"I suppose so. It seems as if I always do."

"You don't make sense, man."

But Pilgrim would die dirty and with all the fancy stuff blown away. He caved in. He begged for a more instant death. A slow bad death made for a slow bad jump. He began to squall when they tied the horses to him to pull him apart.

It isn't as easy as it sounds to distract a man with horses, without distracting him to death. One arm came off, and then there seemed to be nothing to pull against. The militiamen looped the horse ropes around his ankles to rend and split him completely, but they only tore off one foot. They pulled his head off with the horses. It came quite easily. Raffels and Augustine declared Dusmano to be dead, and a militiaman signed chits for them so that they might be paid their stipends.

Dusmano was an untidy scattering of meat, of mud and blood, of dirt and detritus. The militiamen looped ropes around parts of him again, to drag him more, to abrade and separate him further.

"Hold your horses!" Mary Morey called firmly, coming

onto the knoll of the distraction, with her brother following. "We're going with him. Don't let him get too far ahead of us or he'll go into panic. He isn't at his best today, militiamen. When you put in your reports, could you make it seem better than it was? This wasn't one of his better deaths. Now please send us after him as quickly as you can."

"Have you a permit to be killed?" one of the militiamen asked.

"No," Mary said. She hadn't thought to get a permit. Neither had James.

"You can't be killed today, then," the militiaman said. "The office is already closed."

"But he won't know what to do when he wakes up and finds that none of us are there," Mary protested. "He'll panic. He'll go to pieces." Then Mary went into happy laughter about it, realizing that Dusmano was already in pieces.

"We'll waive the permits," a sergeant of militia said. "We'll make this clean and fast." He scored Mary deeply at all the joinings and branchings with a ritual short sword. Then the foamy horses were roped to her extremities and driven with whips and shouts. They lunged and they broke her, and Mary came apart quite easily. Then there was another pulling apart, and still another. The Doctors Raffels and Augustine pronounced her dead and received chits whereby they could collect their stipends.

And her brother James was separated and killed in much the same way. He was not at all a sinewy man, and the horses weren't lathered much more in pulling him apart.

"Anyone else?" the militia sergeant called.

"Yes. I'll have to go with him," Zontik said. "He'll need my umbrella over him wherever he goes. No man ever needed shielding more."

"Do you people have any idea what you're up to?" the sergeant asked, puzzled.

"Not an idea, no," Zontik admitted. "An idea is mental. We have a visceral prompting, perhaps."

They killed Noah Zontik with the horses. Then they killed Doctor Raffels. But Wut in his rage terrified the horses, so he was killed by simple garrote.

Doctor Augustine made his way out of life by private conveyance, after he had collected his stipends, including Raffels's death stipend.

The whole thing was anticlimax without climax.

It is easier for a camel to go through the eye of a needle, than for a rich man to enter into the kingdom of heaven.

Matthew

You know how that camel does it? He just closes one of his own eyes and flops back his ears and plunges right through. A camel is mighty narrow when he closes one eye and flops back his ears. Besides, they use a big-eyed needle in the act.

Narrow Valley

This was in one of the narrow provinces of the country of those who have just died. It was at a place sometimes called the Iron Meadows and sometimes called the Camel's Eye; the most straitened portion of this place was known as the Narrow Corner.

There were three figures coming up the steep, dangerous, and molten path where it climbed toward the Narrow Corner at an angle that sighted into the lowering iron sky above. One of these three had been a powerful cult figure in another place, and now appeared in most peculiar outline. It was not in fuzzy outline; it seemed to be expressed in a number of sharp and clear outlines superimposed. It was like a clear figure seen by double vision, by triple vision, by dozen vision. But no detail of it was smudged.

Thus the creature, according to its various outlines, might sometimes be taken for an ape, at other times a teras, or a Groll's Troll, or a tityrus, or one of the sorts of man, an Enacian, a frog. This pan-morphous creature seemed brittle and unplastic, and yet he could have been manipulated.

The two other creatures coming up the garish, steep, scorching path were an ariel and a dog. These had once been a human brother and sister who had served the first figure in his cult. Indeed, they were still in human form, but the impression they gave was of a dog and an ariel. These two moved with a sort of leashed fury, and all three of the climbing creatures were dangerous and fanged.

Confronting them above were three other figures. One was an ape-shaped human who had once been called the Holy Knacker. One was a wrathy person who in life had born the cognomen of Wut. One was a demented and furious child who, in another place, had been born to parents named Pym.

"Easy, easy," said the climbing ariel in her controlled fury. "Those waiting above are as wary of us as we are of them. We will fill their eyes with murk and be invisible to them. But our eyes will see."

It was a battle for centrality, then. From which boxlike head would which eyes look out to establish themselves as the center?

It was the pan-morphous cult figure climbing up the smoky path from below who won the first slight advantage for his party. The eyes of this pan-morphic (he had jeweled eyes or cracked-glass eyes) established the field of battle and made it conform to their own vision. So those above were purblind and made to move in a private darkness. And yet they were all the sort of beings who work well in the dark.

But this focusing by the cult figure was a distortion and almost unendurable calamity, even to himself. It itself was a wild darkening. Things appeared much more frightening through the eyes and mind of this marred cultist than through the myriad eyes of that personified and spooky place itself. And this more frightening version became the imposed reality both for those below and for those above.

This pan-morphic cultist was himself injured in mind and memory. He was horribly vulnerable through several holes in him. And he could not recall just what these holes meant or where they had been received. He was demented and savage even beyond the sullen savagery of his two servitors, the ariel and the dog. He knew that these two creatures were absolutely faithful to him. But he also knew that they were random and excited and unreasoned, and that their savage faithfulness could as well result in their rending him to pieces (to save his essence by carrying it in their own gullets through the dangerous places) as it could result in anything else. And he was overpowered by the things he saw above him. He knew that when prodigies meet beyond life and time, they are like small boys bluffing each other. He knew that, and he was still overpowered. Small boys bluff murderously when they are removed beyond life and time.

Foremost of the threats was a hulking apelike creature that the polymorph saw high ahead. (This was all by firelight, there being no sun in the iron sky, so the seeing and the seeming ran together.) The ape-thing was moving down the terrible and steep path toward the three climbers. It was coming fast enough to intercept them at the Narrow Corner. The path was fearfully narrow even where the three climbed it. The ariel had her crest drooping and smoking; the dog had his singed tail between his legs; the polymorph himself had teeth in his heart that crunched it and gnawed it away.

And above them, as they climbed, the path fell away much more. It narrowed and vanished off to gnashing horror on each side. How more wonderful it would be if it could be said that it fell away to nothing! But the Narrow Corner, still above them and seeming to loom higher as they approached closer, was snagged, tentacled, pulsating, steep. It was more frightening by much than the torturous path which they were still climbing.

This Narrow Corner was sometimes called "the Camel's Eye," but there was either a mystery or an error in that name. The fable was of the camel and the eye of a needle. Well, but the fact was a giant camel-eye by whose favor this whole cavern existed.

Besides the apelike creature above and ahead, there was a smaller and younger and incomparably more savage being who perched there on a ledge like a bird and who gibbered like the young of the buzzard-bird. This young fury was in open lust for the life and soul of the climbing polymorph. The fury-creature was partly in the form of a rebelling child, partly in the form of a fire-drake, partly in the form of the crackling-voiced buzzard.

But the fury-child, unlike the apelike creature, was not moving down the crumbly, slippery, lava-flow passage. It moved in a different way. It pervaded all that narrow, steep upper wasteland; it pervaded the Narrow Corner itself; and it began to pervade the impossible lower path that looked up past the Corner at the iron sky. This fire-drake, this demented child came to bear on places not by moving from one place to another, but by occupying one place more and another less until it was fully and threateningly in a new place. And this new place might not be exterior to its prey.

> Demons, demons, spew and spree!
> Gouge your eyes out. Count them three.

The smoky stalactites of that passageway rimed the dog-foot verse with limestone and brimstone tone in effective

salure. And above the climbers was seen a third thing or person—a half circle of shaggy darkness opening to show the new one: a madman, or at least an infuriated man. This was an intelligent, calculating, canny, relentless, unforgetting, unforgiving man who had happened to find himself in this unforgivable place and so was possessed by rage and mania.

These were the persons of the three-tiered arena. In addition to them, there were various chimeras, both above and below and in the Narrow Corner itself. They formed a confusing aggregate of persons and players, and it was a confusing and as yet experimental theater in which they played their parts.

(Do not be restless. There is fire everywhere, and your feet will burn off if you take even one step to withdraw.)

There is a legend that comes back from not quite the other side, from the anteroom of beyond, as it has been called. This states that the Narrow Corner is a precipice of glare ice with garish lights rippling over and through it; that this precipice is abrupt as a rough knife-edge; and that on each side of this knife blade there is a howling and bottomless chasm where one may fall endlessly. It states that there are spirits there, unseen (but their frosty breath can be seen against the darkness)—tooth-clattering spirits who are ravening to be eating souls. And it says that all revenges that survive life will wait to be slaked at that Narrow Corner which everybody must pass.

(The dismal child, or fire-drake, was pervading its way nearer and ever nearer.)

And this legend is mostly false, as the climbing pan-morph now understood. Someone, perhaps, had had a visual intuition or prevision of the Narrow Corner, and had believed that it was ice. But it is molten rock and rock crystal, and the garish lights that ripple over and through it are the killing fire. It is a precipice like a knife-edge, yes, and it falls off on each side to unbottomed horror; but the spirits that soar like blood-bats there have their path made visible by flame-breath and not by frost-breath. And the revenges that lurk murderously there do not hide in ice stalagmites but in burning bushes of incandescent iron.

The dismal child or fire-drake was now pervading the very nearness below the Narrow Corner and was attacking the pan-morph, thinly at first, and then more thickly. "I hide in the passage and I trap you there when you have to travel," the demented child sputtered. "There is room for only one on the path, and I'll harry you over the edge, I will shove you over clear to hell. This is the narrow edge, this is the Narrow Corner, this is where I catch you in your fresh death and drive you into steep Tartarus."

The demented child who was also the fire-drake, who was attacking the pan-morph more substantially now, was not clearly visible to the pan-morph. There was one hate-shot child-sized eye riding on the fiery effluvium of the fire-grinder; that alone was clearly seen. The eye was conscious and dripped bottomless hatred. But the members of the child which inflicted horror-touch and wound could not be seen.

But the ariel joined battle with the child fire-drake, and both of them were toothed with slasher tusks. There were hot and bloody doings on those narrow ledges. And from above there came an apish voice like high-pitched thunder.

"I'll chain you to one form," the apelike creature called from above to the assaulted pan-morph. "I'll prison you in only one body, hot ocean-man, change-man, morphic-man. I'll nail you up within your one single flesh and I'll have you stolen completely away from the change-form ocean. Do you not remember me? I was the flesh-smith, the body-smith. But you can't go home again, not to the same ocean bottom, not to Sea-Change Station, which you have depended on. The change you begin now will be your final and straitened form. I narrow it, I restrict it, I nail it up tight. This is your last change, and your new name is 'Change-No-More.' "

The lightning dazzled and the thunder rolled, but neither was absolutely imposing under that low iron sky.

"No, no. There are nine other changes you do not know about," the pan-morph howled. "These are to be left to me after all others except the last one are used up. I have these nine special ones by unusual Legacy. I've tricked you."

"You'll waste the nine; you'll be nine times taken when they're soon over with," the body-smith growled with an animal sound in his throat.

Then it was battle all the way. And the vaunts of the ape-man were a major part of the battle. The animal-man, the ape-man, the flesh-smith, the body-smith was howling his vaunts out of his belly which had been burst. Those vaunts clanged big iron doors shut on last hopes, and they scorched and shriveled.

The Narrow Corner wasn't built by hands, not by flesh hands. It was a projected image that was made solid by its own fire. It was the anthology of thousands of such personal projections. It was influenced, it was even manufactured by the intuitions and projections of countless bruised and dislocated persons in death throes or in death prescience.

There was Alighieri who projected and shaped much of the Narrow Corner. There was Christ in Matthew. There was Maugham. There was mad Blake. There was Anastasia Demetriades who recounted the prophetic frightfulness of the Corner to Count Finnegan who projected it back to the thing itself with his amazing visualization. And clerk Ovyde constructed sheer heights of the Corner by the strong impetus of his Lost Cantos. (They were not lost: they were burned in punishment for their own dangerous clarity.)

These people had shaped the iron rocks of the Narrow Corner; they had instituted the stenches and the heats. And it isn't finished. You'll add to it yourself in your death straits, if there is any deformed originality at all in you.

(Dazzling lightning and rolling thunder again.)

The wrathy man from above had come down onto the terrible, slippery, crumbling Narrow Corner of fire and height. He came to join the assault on the pan-morph, who had begun to clarify out of his ocean of forms. But the wrathy man was intercepted by the servitor dog. And the dog, newly powerful and of a still steeper savagery than before, closed with the wrathy man, intercepting him, fastening into him with sharp iron teeth, shearing off the defending fingers of the maniac, gobbling through gore, eating throat cartilage with clanging teeth. And the maniac man was breaking the neck of the dog, but he would never break that head loose. It was a lightning dog in its dazzling assaults; and the maniac was a thunder-man in his roaring and clattering defiance.

But can lightning and thunder under a low, finite, iron sky be of the same power as lightning and thunder in open infinity? Ah, is the lion less to be feared in a small, closed, entrapping room than on the open savanna?

The battle was on three fronts now. The demented child was no longer the fire-drake. He was the python destroying the ariel. The maniac was fang for fang and torn throat for torn throat with the iron dog, annihilating its flight forever and burning down its mind. The hairy-ape flesh-smith had tangled with the now sea-clarified man, both of them rasping with fright on the slippery lava of the high knife-blade-narrow pass.

Even in death such prodigies as these do not happen. But they happen in that half hour that comes right after death.

It was the dog that went first to falling destruction. The enraged man had broken all four of the dog's legs. He had broken its back and its neck. He had torn out its eyes, and he had smashed its skull, which scrambled its wits forever. But the enraged man could not tear the beast loose from his own throat. When finally the infuriated man flung the broken animal off the knife-sharp ridge, his own torn-out red throat went with it.

And the dog fell through unrecording space that hadn't an end.

The maniac man sank down in voiceless and blood-gushing helplessness. Only his eyes seemed alive now, and they were insane with a new fury. The clarified man from the sea realized that the maniac was the man with the code name of Wut. But who could reap the Wut fortune now?

The dog fell. It was heard to hit the last ledge that marks the underside of the earth. It was heard to scratch and scramble on the hot iron stones of that ledge, and it was heard and felt to fall again. It must have lost the gore-mass from Wut's throat, but it found voice at the same time. Howling in the depths! Deeper and deeper into those depths that are outside of limited space! The voice ever lower in tone but still with sustained strength for a long while! Gone, dog, gone!

The demented child had now left off being a python. It had destroyed the flight of the ariel. It had destroyed her voice and balance and spirit. The ariel fell into the black-wing pit of her enemies, down and down, with the wings torn clear off her. She fell, and her brother, the howling dog, still fell.

But the mad child had now pervaded the higher area and was winking out from the Narrow Corner. He was again no more than one hate-shot child-sized eye riding the effluvium of the burned-out lightning that betrashed the melted iron floor of the Narrow Corner.

The clarified man who had been tricked out of his changing and protecting ocean now knew that the demented child was the younger son of Aubrey Pym, who had gone, throat-cut and trusting, to take a message for a man named Pilgrim Dusmano. But that younger child hadn't gone trusting.

"It must have been a garbled message," the now exundined and single-shaped man said, "with one quarter of it not getting there at all."

"Your two companions and friends have been destroyed into the chasm," the flesh-smith said. "Now you, nailed up tight in a single skin, will follow them. This is the end for you, Mr. Jump-No-More."

"I'll not go into the pit that has no way out." Jump-No-More swore his decision, burying his teeth in the nape of the flesh-smith.

"Ah, but there *is* a way out," the flesh-smith gibed as he tore open the belly of Jump-No-More. (Why did this seem peculiarly vengeful and fitting?) "There is *one* way out, and only one way. And you'll not like that one way, not after you understand what it is. Ah, how is it now, bright man, to be clarified as to form, and to find out you're still made out of mud?"

But the clarified man, Mr. Jump-No-More, was very strong. He could have handled this animal-kin creature, this flesh-smith, if he had had a solid place to stand, if his stomach had not been ripped out, if he were as clarified in mind as he was in form. But his mind still had those superimposed outlines, as though it were a clear mind afflicted by double vision, by triple vision, by dozen vision. He was nearly certain that he had now settled into a human form and that he would retain that form as long as he retained any. But he was fuzzy and witless and confused. He did not fully understand about the Narrow Corner, or he was afraid to understand it. He did not know his own name, nor where he wanted to go or, more important, where he did *not* want to go. It was very important that he arrive at a new place, that he arrive quickly at *any* new place except one.

He bit and gnawed deeply into the nape of his enemy there, and the feet of both of them slithered on the ice-smooth, fire-lava, hog-back, knife-sharp Narrow Corner.

"All results here are final, you know," grunted his pungent, rank-fleshed opponent, this ape-shape, this flesh-smith, this rank and rampant man. "You will go into that pit, man, and there is only one way out of it. Extinction would be better, but you don't deserve so good a thing as extinction." And the lout was pulling the intestines out of the clarified man, out of Mr. Jump-No-More.

"Nothing here is final except your own destruction!" the clarified man sputtered, still grubbing with his teeth in the nape of his enemy. "I avoid all final things forever!" He made a great effort then, and he gained two advantages: he broke his enemy's neck, and he remembered his own name. His name was Polder. He was Polder, that which has been reclaimed from the amorphous ocean, that which has taken solid form and will change no more. Unchanging form is a prison, he knew. But one must give up something to get a name. Oh, the danger of the scuffle there!

There was an old, odd, familiar, remembered-in-exuberance, and yet rather unpleasant odor to this flesh-smith man that Polder was destroying. It was the smell of molten gold, always a foul smell even when one fluxes its melting with lime. Why, this creature was the Holy Knacker himself, and this Narrow Corner was the place where one settles disputes left uncompleted by death! The knacker was a rough-finished man, but not a true ape-form. Where had Polder known him? And how did the fellow happen to smell of a gold that had been melted and reduced with lime flux?

Polder crushed the knacker then with a crunching of bones and a tearing of sinews; and he flung that man into the pit, the abyss where he would fall forever, as the dog had fallen. And then Polder tried to patch up his own belly with the melted rock and melted iron. It wasn't a good job that he did on himself, but it would serve.

Polder reeled on the narrow, knife-blade path. He staggered with the heat, with the stenches, and with the buffets of the black-wings flying above the chasm. He knew that he'd fall. There was no good standing place at all in Narrow Corner.

"All results here are final," the Holy Knacker had said. And Polder slipped and fell finally into the chasm.

But did he fall to his destruction? No, not at all. There was hiatus here. There was a Legacy to account for. There was a bright roll of nine rich lives and worlds which were pleasant little pieces of eternity and which would use up no time at all. There was that string of jeweled worlds of the restrictive covenants.

There was the jump, yes. But then there were the wonderful unclocked times in between. And then—

—the guarantee
From Lambeth that the Rich can never burn,
And even promising a safe return:—
"We let such vain imaginaries pass!"
Then tell me, Dives, which will look the ass—
You or myself? Or Charon? Who can tell?
They order things so damnably in hell.

Belloc

The rich are different from us.

Fitzgerald

There is a compensation and counterpart to the "Eye of the Needle" edict. The rich would not have accepted it without this. The rich have a special Legacy: The Nine Lives to La Spezia. After they die they are permitted to live nine more lives of pleasure almost hysterical in its immediacy and extent before they go to hell.

Clement Goldbeater,
The Enniscorthy Chronicle

It was a Medici who first raised his rich eyes and saw it in the sky, though special persons had been living bright and timeless lives there almost from the beginning. It is right in the middle of the Milky Way and is the most wonderful rivière or litany of jeweled worlds to be found there. Why have vulgar eyes not been able to see it? We don't know this. It is picked out in brilliant midnight-blue light, or three-in-the-morning-blue light for anyone with jeweled eyes to see. There are nine blue-bright stars, each of them illuminated by the light of

one of its own transcendent planets. The rivière of the nine stars or lives is in the shape of a
promontory or cape, and the nine are named
Cannes, Oraioi Polloi, Hy-Brasail, Smart Set,
Savona, Delectable, Theleme, Luogo Perfetto,
La Spezia. It is difficult to maintain historical
calm in recounting them.

Arpad Arutinov, *The Backdoor of History*

The melodious shrillness of Janie's voice, loaded with
musical complaint, drifted into the area. All voices on Cannes
World were melodious and all expression was musical. And
there was no objection to complaint. Complaining was one
of the things they did best on Cannes World.

"You are not using live persons!" Janie shrilled, melodiously of course. "That was a sham Jezebel they used! Get the
Marshal of the Animations!"

The charge, if true, was a serious one. It was required that
live persons be used in all roles at the Cannes Perpetual
Animation Festival.

"Have you evidence? Have you proof?" Pelion called as he
came into the area. "Was anyone watching except yourself,
Janie? Can this thing be verified?"

"Verified, Pelion? There are the pieces of her yet." She
pointed. "There is her head still on the sand. Look at the
blinking blank eyes and the lazy grin still on the face of the
severed head. It's clearly an automation."

"I believe they are already dragging the Marshal of the
Animations here," Pelion said. "Which particular presentation was it, Janie?"

"*Jehu's Companions Finding the Remains of Jezebel,*" Janie
told them. "This is Dore Day, you know. We pay enough.
They're obliged to supply live persons for all the roles."

On Cannes World, the Cannes Perpetual Animation Festival was under way. One of the conditions of there being a Cannes World was that the Perpetual Animation Festival must always be maintained with live actors. On Cannes there were ten thousand dramas a day, for the days were long. There were ten thousand days in a year. There were ten thousand years in a lifetime such as was passed by the elites there. By the end of one such appointed lifetime on Cannes all the great dramas would be fulfilled once. And after that they would repeat, for persons were constantly joining and leaving the life-flow of Cannes.

On this day the dramas were based on the ten thousand best known illustrations of Dore, one of the few laborers who had provided enough basic material to last for an entire day. The drama for this particular period was *Jehu's Companions Finding the Remains of Jezebel.* It was quite a stark presentation. There was a fine and coherent story line, of course, but the main effect of the drama was visual. The body of Jezebel mutilated and broken up into dog-sized pieces, dismembered and thrown to the wild dogs to devour—that was always a good show. The presentation was always by moonlight (yes, certainly a real moon was used in the play), with the top half of the moon blocked out by clouds. The scene was beside a blind-faced stone wall in an obscure part of the city. Two wild dogs had withdrawn a ways at the arrival of Jehu's Companions, but a third wild dog still gnashed at the pieces of Jezebel.

There was a hand of her. There was a foot. Then there was the head lying in a natural position in the roadway and still wearing its coif. And then there was the other hand near the head. There were only four Jehu Companions in the presentation, and there were only those four pieces of the body. Someone had scrimped on the show, but the drama was ordinarily so well done that nobody had protested before. It had the virtue of simplicity.

Each of the four pieces of Jezebel's body asked a riddle, and each of the four Jehu Companions answered it. The first hand asked:

"Who hurls the sin from the synagogues?
Who is it eats me? Who are the dogs?"

And the first Companion answered:

"We the elites with the royal itch.
We are the grand ones. We are the rich."

That appeared to be the correct answer according to the drama. Then the foot of Jezebel asked:

"Who is it casts my flesh for fees?
Who are the sinless s.o.b.'s?"

And the second Jehu Companion answered:

"We are the leaders, we are the ones.
We are the high centurions."

Then it was the turn of the severed head in its coif. And the head asked:

"Who with my common clay makes free
And tramples the dying lumps of me?"

And the third Jehu Companion answered:

"The illumined flesh and the ghosts supreme:
We are the cream of the cream of the cream!"

There was something very powerful in these bloody pieces of Jezebel asking the riddles. After the Jezebel body had been broken up into these handy pieces for the wild dogs to devour, the pieces had been injected with vita-flow to keep them alive enough to talk; but all that was mere stagy detail. But now the bantering verses were building little stair-steps that were the first risers of the climax. And the other hand of Jezebel asked:

"Who is it wages a witless war
And pesters my death in my purgatoire?"

And the fourth Jehu Companion answered relentlessly:

"We are the unrepentent host,
The Legatees of the Azure Coast."

Wait for it; it isn't answered at all. Those were only little dramatic tricks to lull you. For at this point that other hand of Jezebel screamed, and revealed that it was the true head of the dead woman, and that what had been taken for the head was only a piece from the rounder part of the body which had been placed there on the sand and capped with a coif. Then the hand that was the true head spoke again in a saying that revealed that all the answers to previous riddles were mistaken ones. And at the same time this true head answered, the earth began to rumble and to quake, and the climax built like a thunderhead; but it was also at this point that—that Janie—the only watcher, as it happened, at the self-sustaining drama—began to screech that the scattered pieces were artificial and not from a live body. This was scandal.

Many other elite persons had gathered now. The Marshal of Animations was dragged before them with a rope tight around his neck and his tongue protruding.

"Why have you not provided a live actress for this most important role?" demanded Albert Fineface, who was captain of the elites for that day (not a sequence day, a momentum-category day).

The Marshal pretended he could not speak with the rope around his neck and his tongue so swollen and protruded.

"We pay enough for live persons," Fineface barked, and he stabbed the end of the Marshal's protruded tongue with a fine sharp dagger. This pricked the Marshal into words.

"There was no young woman available," the Marshal slavered and sobbed. "You had gone through more than a hundred of them already on the morning of this bloody day. You know that some of the plays were requested to be presented again and again. Of course we have other young ladies coming from the country, as we know that Dore Day is always quite bloody. They will be here almost immediately now. And we have other shipments following at regular intervals. But, well, I miscalculated, and there was no young woman to be had for that brief interval."

"Not even one?" Fineface demanded.

"No, not even one," the Marshal gurgled, "except—ah—not even one."

"Except what?" Fineface roared. "Answer me. We'll have you in dog pieces yourself in a minute. I'll have an answer if I have to pull it out of your throat."

The Marshal would not answer, or it may be that he could not. Fineface reached into the Marshal's throat and pulled out the answer.

"Except my own daughter," was the answer.

Ah, that was the sort of bait the elites could rise to. Oh, they had that Marshal's daughter there soon enough. They ran the drama through again, with the Marshal's daughter in the starring role. And she proved herself to be a fine actress with her vivid portrayal of fear and horror and defiance and other emotions. And she was dismembered quite easily, in pieces handy for the wild dogs, for she was young and tender.

But she departed from the script just when the riddling was lending itself to the climax. Her other Jezebel hand, which was the true Jezebel head, gave a riddle of its own in place of the riddle that was in the scenario. It used other meter and other pace and gave a whining rending:

> "Who thus forgets, in hell or hot:
> No drop of blood will be forgot?"

And the fourth Jehu Companion forgot his lines and said nothing.

A new Marshal of Animations was appointed, and the old Marshal was beheaded and disarmed—one arm here, one arm there, pieces all over for the wild dogs to gnaw. And then the head of the old Marshal rhymed a rhyme that was an unheard thing. There was not even a part written for him in the drama.

> "Who has nine lives that extra be,
> And suffers aye for suffering we?"

It's a good thing they got rid of that old Marshal.

Pelion Tuscamondo was in a bright and breezy seashore booth with Janie, who was his frequent couch companion. Pelion was a handsome man with contoured and flowing fair hair. He had a powerful and carrying voice, but at the same time it was intricate and modulated, almost feminine. He had a shimmer, a dazzle about him. He had been called the hypnotic man, the electric man, the magnetic man, the transcendent man. He was the man with the flowing hands that dripped beneficence. There was the curling and pleasant mockery on his mouth, the incredible vulgarity in the set of his fat jaw, the wild-horse look in his face. And Janie, oh, she was the stereotyped perfection of all the bright women who share in the Legacy.

Pelion and Janie watched eight fine dramas, all based on

great illustrations by the workman Dore: *The Strange Nations Slain by the Lions of Samaria; Babylon Fallen; The Giant Antaeus; The Perilous Pass* (elements from the Pass have gone into the Narrow Corner, you know); *The Mourners of Durandarte; Don Quixote in His Library* (this is a misnamed illustration and drama; it is really God in the throes of Creation, before he learned to delegate the details); *The Panther in the Desert; The Resurrection of Lazarus.* Both Pelion and Janie had jeweled eyes by which they might easily watch eight dramas, and jeweled minds by which they might understand them.

They watched the eight dramas at the same time, then?

No, no, you misunderstand. There is no such thing as "at the same time" on Cannes World, or on any of the Nine Worlds of the rivière or litany, the worlds that comprise the Legacy. The Legacy was not made out of nine segments of time. It had no point of contact with time, so it could never become an elapsed thing. The Legacy consisted of Nine Moments, which is to say nine momentums or powers.

The Resurrection of Lazarus was the best of the dramas: it was always a joy to watch. The Christus would raise him quickly and then be called away on other matters. Lazarus would rise from the dead putrid and thirsty; and putrid he would remain with rotted and half-rotted streaks of flesh, and the more completely rotted pieces sometimes falling clear off of him. And thirsty he would remain, and this was the delight of the whole animation. The elite audience would order cold drink after cold drink to allay in themselves the thirst of Lazarus. The *Resurrection* was always an audience-participation drama.

But Pelion Tuscamondo could hold more than eight attentions in his multiplex mind. This *Resurrection of Lazarus* didn't seem sufficiently researched to his taste. He felt that it needed mountains for its backdrop, and he ordered mountains. He had "Faith Sufficient," and he had station and connections. How could they refuse him mountains?

Albert Fineface, as spokesman for the elites that day, effected the order. And there were mountains, Gothic mountains, Dore mountains, steep menacing mountains, but their spires were twinkling blue instead of midnight black. Lazarus was resurrected in Bethany, perhaps, or in some other small town very near to Jerusalem. And the Anti-Lebanon mountains, or the Hermon or Hauran or some such mountain mass, loomed into the foreground with the breath-catching thrill of very great depth both above and below. And there was very great depth in the resurrected man, depths of thirst and agony.

A cup of water was set before Lazarus. Then, by the power of the group mind of the partakers of the drama, the cup was set out of reach of the suffering man. Once more, small and putrid pieces fell off that good man (where would be the drama in torturing an ungood man?) who did not seem aware of his good fortune in being alive again. With a frantic, animal cry, Lazarus reached mightily for the cup, and the audience-participation group mind moved the cup away from him again.

"It's authentic," Albert Fineface said. "One always experiences intolerable thirst on being raised from the dead. But now, friend Pelion, turn one facet of your jeweled mind to me. You, who have everything, have been wishing for one additional thing; you have not yet formulated this wish well, but you've been wishing it for a long interval. You wish to give testimony of your personal flame and image. As a cult figure, you wish the largest possible publication for your testimony."

"Yes," Pelion declared. "I would like to publish myself in every extent of every ocean that underlies every world. There is a deal to be made somewhere. I've followed some unusual commerces, but I don't know where to make this transaction."

"I can help you," Fineface said. "We've both followed unusual commerces, and we'll let our trading realms intersect here."

The avid crowd with its avid mind power moved the cup just out of the reach of Lazarus again.

This man, Albert Fineface, was a factor in some very dubious transactions, but he did not fail in any of his promises. Should a genie, for his own cloudy reasons, wish to be back in his imprisoning bottle, Albert could arrange it, for a fee. He could fill stranger requests.

"This ocean that underlies every earth," Fineface was saying, "that underlies every creature and manifestation, that infuses every mind and .memory, even the memory of that concocted mountain there, the pervading water that is the uterine as well as the ultimate ocean, this ocean may be suffused as well as suffusing. We will suffuse it with your flame and image. You will publish your testament in every gout of its water. And then you will be permanently in the cellar of every mind that is, and has been, and will be. When a cobwebby bottle is brought up from the cellar of the mind of glowworm or giant, drops of your own flame will sparkle out of that bottle. It will cost you, though. You will buy the pervading water as Lazarus does, but you will buy oceans as he buys drops."

By a dramatic device not immediately explained, Lazarus had mortgaged the livings of his descendants for seven generations, and he had turned it all into mortgage-gold. He was allowed to drop gold coins into the cup of water and to lap up what drops of water overflowed the brim of that cup. But the cup itself seemed insatiable, and it drank up many coins for every drop of water that it brimmed over.

"The recording ocean is known on some of the worlds as the 'Group Unconscious' and on others as the 'Folk Ocean,' "

Fineface was saying, "and any trace of substance in any part of it is immediately in all parts of it. This ocean, as you may not know, Pelion, is made up of the personal testaments of a group of devils. The testaments of these devils may be known and distinguished by their literary or eidetic styles in this repository, which is the most plastic of all the mass (non-lineal, of oblated bulk of mass) media. And each of these testaments receives very wide publication (infinitely wide, in billions upon billions of minds and nexuses); but most of them are without excellence. There are not many (a few more than one hundred) of these testifying devils who have achieved group-unconscious publication. When they were first raveled out and identified by their styles, they were given letters, as 'a,' 'b,' 'c' scrivener or eidetic devil, to distinguish among them. Soon it was seen that the conventional alphabet would not have enough signs. The Tarshish Syllabary was therefore used.

"Symbols of the elements are also used in the latest literary criticism of these authors and creators. It is believed that there will be the same number of these devils publishing their testaments as there are elements in the universes. It is worth noting that the discovery of the nine most recent elements has coincided with the discovery of the nine most recent of the scrivener or media devils. Should you reach this inner circle, Pelion, your equivalent would have to be an unstable element; that's the only kind left."

"I wouldn't want it any other way, Fineface."

"So it's been asked for some time, 'Cannot others play this game?' And we say, 'No way'; we say that if the asker is short of heel. But must it be so restricted? May one not, by fabulous expenditure, buy a membership? May one not buy a pew-stall in this most unchurchly of churches? Yes, I think it may be done. I think it has been done. I believe you or I might be able to do it, Pelion. We are very rich, and we are very flexible in our talents."

"Is it really worth it, Fineface?" Pelion asked. "I don't fund every extravagant idea that comes into my head."

"It will be worth it to you. You will be able to lodge your flame and your image in every mind and every flesh, from the most attenuated flesh to the most gross, from the fire-flame spirit-flesh of the ethereals to the gamy and humpbacked flesh of the camel (your totem animal, is it not, Pelion?). For all of these drink out of that rank-water ocean called the group unconscious, or called other things."

"Other new ones have joined in this?" Pelion asked. "It has been done?"

"Yes, it has been done by several of the Media or Eidetic Lords of various worlds. It has been done by several of the cult figures on and between the worlds."

"With whom might I deal?" Pelion asked. "This is a thing I would like to master."

"Pelion, I can tell you who can tell you who can tell you who. You must pay heavy toll at each station, of course."

"Ah, who can tell me who can tell?" Pelion asked.

"Oh, I can." Albert Fineface made ready for the commerce.

So Pelion paid him very heavy toll and was on the way to contrive entrée in and influence on the inmost under-minds of all creatures and uncreatures, living and dead. When one is "in" there, one is in forever.

The cup from which Lazarus sought to drink developed a deep crack from the weight of all the heavy gold coins placed in it, and all the water ran out of it. It was a badly built cup. And Lazarus moaned with his mouth in the sand.

(A nonessential change in worlds and lives and persons happens here.)

Nine worlds unto satiety
Of joy unending till you hate it,
Nor any way to cool it be,
Nor any way to terminate it.

Endymeon Ellenbogen, Arena del Mar

"There's an umbrella salesman waiting to see you, Pelion," Janie said.

"I'll catch him on the next world," Pelion-Palgrave said. "I've got to go now."

"All right. I'll tell him," Janie-Jeanie said.

He did not go, of course. There is no going from any of those places ever. A particular scanner may leave him there and focus on someone else in some elsewhere; but there was no way that Pelion Tuscamondo could ever leave.

The Nine Lives to La Spezia are not over with. They are still going on; they go on forever. Remember when you are in hell that there are still nine other versions of you enjoying the nine lives of almost intolerable pleasure and enjoying it forever. It is always a cooling thought, and they can't take it away from you.

But what have certain sets of persons in common? What have Pilger Tisman, Pilgrim Dusmano, Pelion Tuscamondo, Palgrave Tacoman, Paladin Tajiman, Polycletus Tasman, Palmas Thasomen, Paulus Theissmand, Pilatus Dosmens, Philemon Dorsetmoon, Philip Dusselmon, Polder Dossman, and so many others to do with each other? What, for that matter, have Janie, Jeanie, Joanie, Junie, Ginny, Jenny, Johnnie, and so many other couch companions to do with one another? Are all of each set the same person?

Let us be careful here; all of us have to live on all these worlds sometime (we are all elites when the elite number of the nine-sided die-cube comes up for us). We cannot discuss here just what a person does consist of; the pillars would split and the roof would fall down on our heads if we did.

All these of the same set are of the same complex; certainly they are all persons of the same complex. There are some very different persons within some of the same complexes (as you understand persons, as you understand complexes). There may, for example, be one saint among many sinners in a complex. This has advantages. You just think you can't get a drink of water down there in the fires of Jehol. You can if you have one accepted saint in the complex of your personality. You can slake your perishing thirst now and then.

(The death thirst, the hell thirst, the Lazarus thirst continued. Only the play and the people in and out of it, and the world, were changed. We'll come back to that thirst.)

But nobody ever uses up the Nine Lives to La Spezia. They are there forever: Cannes, Oraioi Polloi, Hy-Brasail, Smart Set, Savona, Delectable, Theleme, Luogo Perfetto, La Spezia. Now the focus is on Oraioi Polloi, and Palgrave Tacoman is at leisure in a loge with a couch companion named Jeanie and with Albrecht Fairbrow. There was an umbrella salesman waiting, but menials must always be kept waiting a bit.

This was Hieronymus Bosch Day. Did Bosch ever paint a *Resurrection of Lazarus?* It's not known; but he did paint *Thirst,* again and again. And perishing thirst was on the boards at the Atrium Theater in Oraioi Polloi. The arrangement of all these living theaters of the Nine Worlds to La Spezia was a geometric one in which every point was but slightly removed from the center.

This is sometimes the arrangement to be found in Adobe Pueblos, where the arena and the village and the world are identical. It is to be found in Ghetto Complexes and in Hogan's Alley arrangements. It is found in Courtyards, on Blocks Facing Inwards, in West Side Story sets. Tomorrow, as a matter of fact, will be West Side Story Day at the Atrium Theater in Oraioi Polloi. This communicating set is destroyed by wide and heavily trafficked roads running through it, but it is not destroyed by alleys or footpaths. It is the archetypical arrangement for dream presentations: all the world watching and aware; and it was the arrangement here.

"Don't buy it, Palgrave," the umbrella salesman said suddenly and rudely. "You'll pay too much to become an archetype."

But he was the man named Lorica. Why had Janie said that he was an umbrella salesman? Why had Jeanie said it? And why had Palgrave himself known it of the man when it wasn't so? For Lorica was one of the elite, and an adept and powerful man in his own right. He sold worlds and systems and whole galaxies. He didn't sell small notions, though he did now have the air of a man trying to sell a notion. And how would there be an umbrella salesman on Nine Worlds, where the weather was completely controlled and localized and individualized?

"You are a good man, Palgrave," Lorica said as though he

had been commanded to say it but didn't quite believe it. "I am commanded to effect it that you be a good man; and I say you are; but you aren't. You already have your fragmented existence in thousands of minds besides your own, and you are of evil effect in those minds. Do not move in to have existence in billions of minds. There are devils enough without you. No good man (Rotten thunder take it! The instructions *say* that you must be a good man!) will go to live in the pit that is under the worlds, or to manipulate in the pit that is under the minds."

"Lorica is a donkey," Fairbrow said with that easy urbanity that is part of the equipment of all deeply evil men. "In the underlay, the pit that is under the worlds and under the minds, is to be found all power and influence. The gold-symbol demon Aurelion is pushing your application for membership in this always exciting and ever new cartel that *creates.* You have the chance to become the substance that men and minds and worlds are made out of. Dare to create!"

"Fairbrow is right," the Putty Dwarf stated. "All things in all worlds are putty in our hands when we become part of the great creative ocean. Dare to be exciting!"

"Faugh!" Lorica snorted. It sounded like an umbrella being let down.

"Lorica is common. He is in trade," the Putty Dwarf said. "He really does sell umbrellas. Has an umbrella peddler the key to the power of the universes?"

"Pay no mind to these mangy mice, Palgrave," the man Lorica said; but the damage was already done to Lorica. "There is opportunity, there is newness, there is excitement, there is real creativity running through all the worlds. The spirit moves. And these gnawing mice of the under-minds know nothing at all about the new things. Great happenings are few, Palgrave. Life happened to matter once; that was a great thing. Transcendence is happening to life now; that is another great thing. Be a part of it."

But there was a cheap echo in Palgrave's mind: "Lorica is an umbrella peddler."

"Antilife happened to matter once," said the Putty Dwarf. "That was our kind of thing. And now something analogous is happening to our valued antilife. This is where we live. All new things begin at the bottom. Dare to be a part of the bottom!"

"What Lorica offers you is free," Fairbrow pointed out. "Can anything good be free? But what we are urging you to strive for—and it's not at all certain you will be able to reach it—is very expensive. The gold-symbol demon Aurelion insists on a huge payment right now. Then he will push your application a little harder. Is not the great cost a proof of the value?"

"Aye, men pay a high price to get into hell," Lorica jeered. "They make application and they politick to get there. It is the shriveling madness."

What petty minds these umbrella peddlers do have! Palgrave gave the order to pay the sum to the devil-angel Aurelion, the seventy-ninth of the recording spirits. It would be simony well spent, whether a membership was obtained or not.

"There is an ariel and a dog here to talk to you," Jeanie said.

"They cannot be the real ariel and real dog," Palgrave contradicted. "They could not be on Nine Worlds at all. They're common. And they're time-chained. They'd never reach to here."

"They are the real ones," the man Lorica said. "I know them. They've come to look after you."

"Quiet, umbrella peddler," Palgrave growled. "I'm not needing any of you here."

"Nevertheless, they want to see you and talk to you," Jeanie insisted.

"I won't talk to them. Why should I talk to an ariel and a

dog? I'll look at them from this distance." And Palgrave Tacoman looked at them.

"They're devoted," Jeanie said softly. "They want to look after you. That's what I want to do also. Listen to them. Listen to me. Listen to this man Lorica."

"No. I'll listen to nobody. I'll speak to everybody instead, pervasively and from underneath. The ariel and the dog are waiting in the field by the horse coursing place."

The ariel was in sunlight. She was freckled and unaccountably brilliant. She was dappled and sunbeamed. She was daylight itself, freckled daylight with clouds roiling up behind her.

And the dog was in shadow. He was a human-form dog. This dog was always somber and silent in the shadow. And it was believed that he was faithful.

"The two of them would be good at coursing big game," Palgrave said. "She in the sunlight, he in the shadow. Let us go coursing then. What game will it be? The tiger won't course. It is sabered, but it skulks in sedge and reeds that are more black than orange. The lion won't course. It suns itself in tawny grass and on yellow rocks. Then it vanishes, or it strikes. The buffalo will course, but only for a while. Then it is into deep mud, and it's a mucky business to drive it out with hound or lance.

"But I know a large and sabered animal that *will* course. Let the tall horses be brought. We'll have a hunt full of bristled death."

A dozen tall horses were brought for a dozen of the elites who would go hunting. A dozen long lances with authentic bogus-stone lance heads were brought. The post boy began to play fanfares and caracole tunes on a long brass horn. This horn was chased with hunting scenes in living color and stunning detail. One of the hunting scenes showed Palgrave Tacoman down on the ground and a giant boar killing him with its sabered tusks.

"That boar does not kill me fairly," Palgrave protested. "The detail is wrong. Change that scene for another."

"That isn't easy," the post boy said with a little shudder. "To change so completed a scene as that would drain me of every power."

"Be drained, then," Palgrave ordered him. "Do it."

The post boy changed the scene on his long horn. The figures writhed and altered and mutated. The boy did drain himself of all strength for the new animation. The new scene showed Palgrave on horseback, and the horse itself being lifted and tossed high into the air on the sabered tusks and huge and bristled snout of a truly giant boar. It was a more brightly colored and more finely detailed scene than the first.

The post boy lallygagged and retched and trembled like a pale specter. It was a strong picture full of fountained blood and crawling flesh. The boy was emptied of strength and blood, and almost emptied of life. It was partly his own blood that colored the gory scene on the horn.

"So that's the way it will be just before the end of it," Palgrave commented. "I feel the authenticity of it. I am not sure I can avoid being destroyed as climax. Leave it as it is, boy; it's well done."

The dog in human form had assembled nine hound-form dogs and had gone into the bosky shadows to drive out whatever rampant animal he could find there.

The ariel had gathered two dozen young peasant girls and lads and was leading them, fear-speckled and excited, down the sunny aisles of the coursing place to rout out all furred and bristled animals.

Flocks of green parrots flew above the gathering fray, whistling, hooting, and giving advice from their level of vantage. There has always been close association between the privileged elite and the parrot flocks.

The dozen elite men and ladies mounted their tall steeds.

"Blow the 'Giant Overture,'" Palgrave ordered the post boy. "Blow it to ensure that all our quarry may be giant. Drain yourself again for the blare."

"They have just discovered—no, they have just manufactured a new element," the pale horn boy told Palgrave Tacoman. "I thought you'd be pleased to know it." But Palgrave didn't understand, for the moment, the meaning this news had for him.

"Blow the 'Giant Overture,'" he ordered, more sharply this time. The post boy blew the giant notes so powerfully as to split the ears of all the mounted elites and send the delightful blood gushing down their faces and necks. It was the first blood to be poured out in that day's coursing.

A very large black boar had been stirred out right on the rich border between sun and shade, between grass and brush. It stood as tall at the shoulders as did the tall horses.

"Take it, Lorica," Palgrave cried. "It's a third-grade boar for a scared and scruffy umbrella peddler."

"This boar would not be third-grade in any world of any universe," Lorica swore.

All the riders joined in at coursing the boar. Hunting the bristled bravos with lance is one of the finest of all pleasures, so long as one does not live by it as a trade.

Parrots were like flights of fat green arrows in the air. Dogs had a catchy bark on every gasping breath, but this boar was not winded by a long and furious coursing. It doubled back repeatedly on small razor feet and huge haunches. It was quick. It had the red light of murder in its warty red eyes. It sounded!

And there came a more rampant and more powerful sounding from the cedared mountain. It was a champion coming to enter the lists of the bristled brotherhood.

But the present and embattled boar wheeled again and killed several of the harrying peasant girls and lads. It left them awkwardly broken in the sunny grass. The boar coursed again, and it foamed, not with weariness, but with fury.

Lorica, on a steep bay horse, closed in on the boar and let his horse overrun itself and become impaled on the wheeling boar. At the moment of overrunning, Lorica's lance went into the boar in snout and mouth and throat, but the bogus-stone lance head did not touch the boar brain in any way. That animal, disdaining even to notice the lance, was into the horse with long tusks, richly and redly into the belly; and it raised horse and rider high into the air as it reared on giant bristled hams and small feet.

Lorica, quickly clear of the saddle and standing high on the fore-shoulders of that death-struck horse, thrust downward powerfully with the lance, and it was clear through the boar. The boar was spitted clean, if he only knew it.

Then the whole construct—boar, horse, rider—fell like a crashing tower; and the man Lorica stepped clear from the two dead animals.

"Good kill," said Albrecht Fairbrow. But Palgrave had no words of congratulation for the umbrella peddler.

Very quickly then, as though some hunt master had been arranging it, another boar was rousted out of the black-shade borders of the hunting course. The new boar sounded immediately. And immediately there was a strong answering sounding from the cedared foothills. The king boar, the champion boar, was coming rapidly. But a near champion was here already.

This boar of record was stronger, faster, probably heavier, not quite so tall as the first one had been. It quickly set up a howling and screaming trail of wounded and broken dogs in the brakes. It was leaving no enemy unbloodied.

It came into the sunlit coursing alleys. It was as truculent a tusker as had ever been encountered. It sent a surge of fear through all the horses, through all the dogs, through all the young peasants. It nearly sent fear through the elites themselves, were they not, by definition, immune to fear.

"Take it, Fairbrow," Palgrave said. Ah, this was the awkwardly dangerous boar that nobody wanted to tangle with. It hadn't the fine lines of the real champions. It hadn't the style. It had an unheroic, hunching, scurrying, very rapid way with it, and it called out an unheroic response in everyone in its path. But the scurrying boar was strongly aware of Palgrave Tacoman.

And Palgrave was now aware that his own cranky testament had been multiplied a billionfold. The post boy, the horn boy, had said that a new element had just been discovered or synthesized. And that new element had to be the correspondence to himself. He knew now that he had been accepted into the unstable-hundred company of the archetypical devil-angels. He knew that his testament, with its new bristle-boar motif, had now become a part of every pool of that ocean named the group unconscious, that it would be dipped into by every thirsting spirit of human or beast or bird or bug, or unbodied flit-brain, or stick or stone or tree or hill. Now he was one of the communicating gods of the atomic numbers, an unstable god of an unstable element. His testament, with its old humpback-flesh camel motif, was already at work in the under-minds of the very grass that his horse trod.

He knew that in the psychology books of all the worlds there had appeared a new archetype. With Imago Dei, with Orpheus, with Child Hero, with Kore there was a new arrival. With Corn-Mother, with Fenris-Wolf, with Hermaphrodite, with Python there was a new lodger in Domdaniel, the castle that is under the ocean. With Black-Beard, with George-and-Dragon, with Helen, with Houri there was a forever-person of the camel totem. One more had joined the most select company of Simon Magus and Baubo and Demeter, of Adonis and Alexander and Broom-Witch, of Leviathan and

Hermes and Homunculus, of Moloch and Fisherman. There was a new oceanic companion to Huracan and to Beggar-King and to Gyne Peribebleene-ton-Helion (Woman Wrapped-in-the-Sun). With the Leper, with the Boogerman, with Body-and-Blood Giant there was now the Palgrave.

Palgrave had gained swift status as a cult figure.

But he knew too that something was gaining on him.

The scurrying boar, coming around quickly, broke the legs from under Fairbrow's horse. The boars of this place were larger and more powerful than bulls. Fairbrow was on his feet and away from his wailing horse. He set himself to face the erratic boar with lance, on foot. And everybody watching knew that Fairbrow was already as bad as dead.

The lance was too long. Or the powerful and short-coupled boar turned on too short an arc. That boar was greased lightning indeed, leaving more grease than blood on the lance head as Fairbrow failed again and again to get a holding thrust into the beast. Then the boar was inside the sweep of the lance. Fairbrow was down. And then he was dead. It was the exact scene that had been on the post boy's horn before Palgrave had ordered it changed. Even the face of dead Fairbrow looked at least as much like Palgrave's as like Albrecht Fairbrow's.

"Will you finish the beast, Palgrave Tacoman?" Leslie Whitebread called. Whitebread seemed to have become that day's spokesman for the elites immediately on the death of Fairbrow.

"I will not," Palgrave called back. "I'll have no man's leavings."

Palgrave was clearly afraid of that arrant boar. "Fairbrow doesn't make a very good Adonis," Palgrave said then with jerky contempt, "and the boar doesn't make a very good Aphacan Boar."

The boar had to be killed by a committee. There are a few

things that a committee can do well. There are very many more things that a committee will always do badly. And killing a boar is one of the things that no committee should ever try at all. There was much additional blood shed on the grassy course, royal elite blood and ignoble boar's blood. Even when he was dead, that rogue boar seemed by the set of his ears ready to clatter back to his feet and resume the fray.

But the king boar was arriving, sounding and trumpeting, from the mountain. Palgrave would have a grander and more heroic beast to battle, but he feared it less than he had feared that scrambling and unpredictable boar that had just been ineptly done to death by a committee.

Now the king boar stood erect and high headed at one end of a mile-long coursing alley. It was a bestial and outstanding red brown fire against the soft blue foothills of the cedar mountain. Palgrave Tacoman, at the other end of the mile-long coursing alley, raised his lance in very high salute. The boar flashed his tusks like white and gold fire in the sun; it was the answering salute. This encounter was heroic, as the previous encounter of Fairbrow and the rogue boar had not been.

Palgrave on his high golden horse set to rush down the coursing alley, and the king boar was coming to meet him in a swirl of royal swinish thunder. There must be only one violent momentum and clash in such an afternoon of champions. Anything else would be repetition, and a grand climax will tolerate no second presentation.

Here was the engraved scene which was bloodily alive for all that: Palgrave on horseback, and the horse itself being lifted and tossed high into the air on the sabered tusks and the strong and bristled snout of the king boar of all Aphaca. Then the scene was full of fountained blood and crawling flesh.

Palgrave had already seen this death of his, in the brazen

horn of the post boy. He had wondered whether he could avoid being destroyed as climax. He couldn't.

Palgrave Tacoman lay in ritual death on the green and scarred and cloven grass of the course. In his death, Palgrave *did* make a very good Adonis. And the boar did make a very good Aphacan Boar. The beast knelt beside Palgrave. It was lance-bit and blooded, but it may not have knelt from blood loss.

At that very moment the "Adoration of the Boar," based on the great painting of Hieronymus Bosch, was being presented as the drama of record at the Atrium Theater there on Oraioi Polloi. But did the boar that had killed Palgrave actually adore him in death? Possibly it did. The boar had a strong sense of ritual.

"The dead Palgrave had an ariel and a dog attending him," Jeanie said to Leslie Whitebread, who had become that day's spokesman for the elites. "What shall we do with them?"

"Whip them and send them away," Whitebread answered.

Death on any of the Nine Worlds was a pleasant coma. There was enough of awareness; there was enough of emanating power and influence. It was a vital and sparkling repose. Everything is always pleasant on Oraioi Polloi, whether in full life or in death-coma. But the focus of attention does tend to veer away from a man after he is dead, even if he is so pleasantly dead as was Palgrave Tacoman.

And associate aspects of Palgrave were pleasuring themselves and thriving on all the Nine Worlds to La Spezia. These are things that do not end. They are going on now. They will still be going on when suns of lesser places run down and die.

But in other and starker places, there are very much ruder things going on. These things are in harsh time, and they can come to abrupt end or to very much worse term than an ending.

12

I'll tell you a story about Mary Morey
And now my story's begun.
I'll tell you another about her brother,
And now my story is done.

Woolly Camel Book of Nursery Rhymes

There had been the jump, yes. But then there had been the wonderful unclocked worlds in between, which are still going on, in a sundered-off place that nobody can visit twice. And then—

—the jump forgets its interval, and the focus is on another and starker place. The stark place is real, whatever fancy context may have been framed for the fancier worlds.

He awoke, with a horrible thirst, on a ragged hillside. Ants were stinging him, but they were small and short-toothed ants. When he sat up his face was raked by thorns. There was a scrawny patch of them there, and it was long past green-thorn time. He had, as he believed, an ariel lying at his head and a dog lying at his feet. From a brindled sky a Hand of Heaven was pointing down at him most effectively.

His name was Polder Dossman, which means "Sleep-Man Reclaimed from the Ocean." But it also means "Toss-Like-a-Bull-Man Reclaimed from the Ocean." He thought of himself more as the horned-bull man. It was a new name to him, one that he had not used before; and he hadn't explored all the sides of it. He had apparently made a successful world-jump. Somehow it had been a rough passage, though.

"Which is my right hand and which is my left?" he cried out in the first words he had ever used in that place. "Oh, why are they continually changing them?" This confusing of the right hand and the left is a disorientation that often plagues jump-travelers.

The Hand of Heaven pointing down was a bit of meteorological manipulation, but he couldn't remember contracting for it. Someone brought him a curious cup that was filled with either green coconut milk or green camel milk. He drained it off noisily, and it took the screaming edge off his thirst.

Polder didn't know where he was and he didn't believe it mattered. He had a way with worlds and with situations. He could have his will with any world, and he could have it with this scurvy one.

"This isn't hell," he said with confidence. "Why should it be? The odds are billions to one against my ever hitting on that one. No, this is just another of those oyster worlds which I with the sword of my wits will open.

"Up, ariel! Up, dog!" Polder cried then with a show of the energy he hoped to acquire. In reality he was sick and tired. He was suffering what some world-jumpers call the "Resurrection Blues." "We have a new world here, I believe," he said as to that world in condescendence, "or at least we have a new slant, or a new shape to live in. It's weed-grown and it's stark, but I will have my will with it. Say, is not the sun bright and beamy where it breaks through the cloud so suddenly now?"

"Hot," said the ariel. "Hot clouds and hot sun. I freckle badly in that combination. I'll bet it's an unconditioned world, except maybe on the rich men's estates. Why ever did we come to a world like this one?"

The ariel had had the wings pulled off her somewhere, possibly at "the Camel's Eye." There was a smoky memory of an encounter at a narrow place named the Camel's Eye. There had been a dismal child or a fury-child that tried to revenge itself for its own murder. There had been a body-smith or knacker with a new passion for unshaping bodies. There had been hot iron ledges that hung over the mouths of pits, and there had been utter destruction below. There had been other prodigies. There had been a clarified man ("Possibly myself," Polder said); there had been a madman named Wut.

"But all those were things that happened to other people, not to me or mine," Polder protested, and he made, for practice, an old and eloquent gesture with his hands.

"But there *are* no other people!" he cried then. "There are a dozen or so people. That is all. And they are repeated billions and billions of times."

The Nine Worlds to La Spezia, whether or not he had experienced them, left no memory in Polder Dossman. Only things that are in past time can leave memories, and the Nine Worlds were outside time.

The unwinged ariel looked very much like a girl of the ordinary sort. She was a freckled, rusty-haired, fair-sized girl in unworried confusion. And she had flat eyes. Hadn't her eyes once been live-sculpted in high relief?

"Why don't you send the Hand of Heaven away?" she

asked Polder. "The people here aren't likely to be impressed by it. And the manifestation must use a lot of power."

"Of course the people here will be impressed by it," Polder said. "I don't remember what sort of contract I made for the Hand, or with whom. I'll not send the Hand away, for I intend to use it again and again. But I'll put it on standby for now."

Polder ordered the Hand onto standby. The light went out of it, so that it could hardly be seen. It was like trying to see a close-orbiting planet in the daytime. It could still be seen, barely, if one knew where to look. But it wasn't effective.

Polder found heavy gold in every pocket. It pleased him that he had remembered to bring it. Gold will sometimes work like a real charm on a strange world; and then again it will often cost one his life if he divulges its possession too soon and too openly. But it is better to have it than not to have it.

"Look how sharp every line is here," Polder exclaimed. "There's no texture to things here; there's no deep pile to confuse us. It's as though it were all drawn with straightedge and French curve. It's sharp-lined in perspective and sharp-lined face on. Notice how clear and sharp are the hills, the trees, the stones!"

"Bloody sharp," the dog grumbled. The dog had a witless way about him. Someone had scrambled his brains forever. He had dog eyes. He had dog whiskers. He was a young man, though, of willing but slow ways; he was a dog only in a fancy manner of speaking. And previously he had been a dog in only one special instance.

The young man had cut his foot on a marvelously sharp stone and was bleeding freely. Polder noticed that the blood was expressed in fine, sharp, black, parallel and very-close-together lines. The fine lines gave good contrast with the white-base world background. The name of this visual aspect of the blood was red, of course; but red should have meant a deeper quality of which the lines were only a token.

And anywhere else than here the lines would have been less sharp; they would have made up a shading or hatching. But there was a missing quality in it all. The name of the missing element was red, just as the name of the token lines was red; but what was that quality really? One who has really seen red, whether in this context or in some other, cannot be flubbed off by even the finest lines or shadings. There were worlds that had color, and there were worlds that only said that they had color. Polder could not quite recall the quality of color to his mind, and the absence of it depressed him.

The girl, who was still an ariel internally perhaps but not in present outward appearance, was named Moira Mara. The other kids must have jazzed her about so odd a name when she was younger. The wan-wit young man, he who had had his brains scrambled while he was still a dog in that dog-passage, was named Jake Mara, and he was brother to Moira.

"We have to watch over you and take care of you," Moira Mara told Polder. "We must do this with utter devotion and complete self-denial. We don't really want to do this, but we are compelled to."

"Who compels you?" Polder asked.

"We don't know," Moira said. "We'd like to get out of it but we can't."

Polder and his two young companions went down the hill to the sharp-line world, to the simple world, to the easy-to-take-advantage-of world. They came to the edge of a little town at the bottom of the hill. People were lounging about; or they were gazing out of their heads; or they were talking to each other. Some of them were working. It seemed to be easy and archaic work, and it had to do with cultivating the land.

But all these people were of sharp and simple and single

outlines. They were clearly people who had never traveled, people who had never balked or mutated, people who had never jumped at all—in body or in shape or in world. They were people who had never realized their concentric aspects, who hadn't mutualized or enriched their personalities, who had not pluralized themselves at all. Further than that, they were so sharp-line that they might have been cartoon characters inked by an open-faced folk artist who himself had never traveled or mutualized or enriched or pluralized.

And yet they were skeptical-looking lads at the bottom of the hill there. To impress them, Polder activated the Hand from Heaven pointing down at him from the sky. Polder was surprised that he knew how to activate it. And the lads were impressed.

"It'd cost more to run that for one minute than I'd make in a lifetime," a live-brained young man said. "Would it cost much extra to fly the wording 'This is My Beloved Son' in daylight flame above it?"

"Yes. It would almost double the cost," Polder said. "I decided against that." He was surprised at the accurate understanding that the young man had for the cost of the meteorological manipulation. He was rather proud of the giant Hand pointing him out.

"What is the name of this village?" Polder asked that brightest-looking of the lads, the one who had admired the Hand from Heaven.

"This is Camel Town. It is the second-best town in the world in every way." The young fellow spoke the words with a grin on every one of them. Was he joking?

"Make a note to find out whether there is humor on this world," Polder told Moira. "Make a permanent note to find that out, almost the first thing, on every new world that we come to. Knowing a little thing like that can often make a difference."

And then he spoke to the young lad again. "If Camel Town

is the second-best town in this world, which is the best? And why has a bright lad like you not gone to the best town?"

"There is no one town that is the best in everything," the lad said. "There are ten thousand different towns (actually there are one hundred and five towns on this world, but ten thousand is a more resounding number), each of them the best in the world at some one thing. But Camel Town, best in nothing, is second-best in everything. It reminds me of people. Now of all creatures, people—"

"Oh?" Polder asked. "Camel Town is second in everything? What a humpbacked idea!"

"Yes, like the camel. The camel is second-best at everything."

"Impossible, lad."

"Everything, sir, absolutely. As a steed, the camel is second-best to the horse. As a pack animal, it is second-best to the jenny-ass. As a draft animal, it is a close competitor to the ox. As a canal-tow animal, it is mighty near as efficient as the Urdu water buffalo. As a plow animal, it gives place only to the mule. As a treadmill animal, it is right behind the hinny."

"Invest in hinnies, Moira," Polder ordered. "A million piasters or so. We've been neglecting hinnies."

"Oh, all right," she said.

"As a threshing floor animal, the camel is not quite equal to the zebu-ox," the lad went on. "At night-song, it's but a shade inferior to the Moroccan jackass. As a companion, the dog alone is in better accord with man."

"Are these certified ratings?" Polder asked.

"Oh, no. We wouldn't even know how to go about certifying them," the lad said. "And then consider the products and by-products of the holy camel! For the making of bagpipes, the stomach of the camel is but slightly inferior to that of the Irish elk."

"Invest in bagpipes, Moira," Polder ordered.

"All right," she said. "We'll blow a bit on bagpipes."

"At butter, the camel is rated right after the yak," the lad told them. "And from the bones of no other animal except the caribou can better buttons be made. A whistle made from a camel's thorax has a tone that is second only to that from the thorax of the bull moose. The buttermilk of the cow-zebu is superior to a camel's, but it's a close contest. Hard cheese from the mountain goats and soft cheese from Cappadocian ewes are the best in the world, but in each case our friendly camel comes near after. The camel's eyeball will ward off the evil eye nearly as well as will that of Wanwanker's wildebeest. Felt from the hair and the fur of the castor-beaver is only a slight bit better than that from the camel. Fleece! Only that of the right ram surpasses that of the camel!"

"Procure me a mantle of right ram fleece, Moira," Polder ordered. "It will always look good, and I bet it gets cold here in the evenings."

"All right. I'll get one with a purple trim," Moira said. "That goes well with a holy or royal image."

"Gelatin from the Bushman gnu, glue from the horse stallion, they are nonpareil," the lad said challengingly. "But in each case the camel product is but a fraction behind. Hair from the musk ox is unequaled for its fineness; but you must remember that camel's hair was used for the original camel's hair brushes when the musk ox was still hardly known. The hide of the cape buffalo is tougher than slate shingles and more flexible than water; but we all know who is number two. Lamp oil? No, the camel can't compete with the whale there, but no other creature on earth can compete with the camel. And as to flesh-meat, the mutton-type meat from the haunches and legs of the camel is outranked only by the flesh of the tup-sheep; the fine, beef-type cuts from the camel's rib cage and trunk are bested, by only one rib-width, by the meat of the yearling steer. The juicy, pork-taste roasts from the camel's hump are out-tasted by the flesh of the fat hog, and by nothing else. Foal's liver is best of all, but everybody knows that camel's liver comes next. For marrow-soup, the bones of the red elk are always best-of-show, but your friendly camel wins place."

"Moira, before I forget it," Polder ordered, "go rent a good grotto for a cult place. And find out what is the leading cult here, besides my own. Discover, if you can, what name my vestigial cult travels under here, and make contact with whatever members of my cult you can discover. This is a patsy world, I suspect, and it is coming onto patsy-picking time. Here I will hang my hat; here I will wage commerce, here on this world. Take enough gold, Moira. Buy anything that looks promising."

"All right," said Moira Mara.

"Cow milk is better than camel milk?" the lad asked rhetorically. "Yes, it is. But really there's no more than a drop-in-a-bucket difference between them. For mohair and angora there is no beating goats; but remember that it takes twelve angora goats to equal one camel in quantity. Neat's-foot oil? Well, the camel must give way to the neat there, but old second-place camel oil is my own soothing favorite.

"Parchment! Fine split lambskin is paramount for good writing parchment, but camel parchment has served for the writings of some of the holiest prophets of them all. For rawhide, there is nothing so raw as a good Cactus County steer; but after this steer, the camel is the rawest animal on earth. For the best rennet, housewives go direct to the cow-calf's stomach; but try to get one to switch who has gotten used to the camel. Shammy skin from the chamois-antelope will put a shine on the whole world, but men were shining with the pliant belly-skin of the young camel before the first chamois was knocked off the first alp. The Cordovan kid produces the best cordovan leather; but, excepting in color, camel-cordovan is absolutely equal to it. Best vellum is from the female kid of the Arcadian goat; second-best is from the camel that has suffered from, but not died of, the mange."

"Jake, go see if you can locate a good umbrella merchant," Polder told Jake Mara, whom he sometimes thought of as a dog. "I always feel better when I know there's one around."

"Yes, I know where to find one," Jake said. "I believe he already has you under survey. He's quite near."

"Yogurt, in strength and authority, is best from the milk of the khudi-cow," the local lad was saying. "And second-best is yogurt from the milk of a camel. Sea lion ribs are most apt of all for tent pegs, but next after them are camel ribs. For the scapula, the shoulder blade bones on which ritual formulas and recipes may be written, the giraffe is in first place by virtue of the sheer length of his bones. But talk to a quality scapula man, and he will talk camel quality. And as to fuel, why, camel manure is a very close second to elephant hokey. For human friendship, the camel averages nearly as high as does man. I could demonstrate my points further."

"What do you do for a living, lad?" Polder asked this youngling.

"I sell camels," the lad said.

"Come work for me."

"Buy my last camel and I will."

"Give him a camel's worth of gold, Moira," Polder ordered. And she did so.

"You remind me of somebody else, of an older man," Polder said.

"Perhaps I've been renovated," the lad answered him. "Most likely I've been an older man at some time or other."

Yes, there was a duplicity of outline about this lad, though it hadn't been apparent before. He had traveled: not so much as Polder had, of course, not so much as a really seasoned traveler, but the lad had traveled.

"I've been waiting for you, you know," the lad said.

"What? Waiting for me today?" Polder asked him.

"Waiting for you for many days, for a year, for three. You've been outside of time, so it may be that you haven't realized how much time has passed. I will have to look out for you and to intervene for you."

"My brother and I will do that for Mr. Dossman," Moira said reproachfully.

"You two, yes," the lad agreed. "But myself also. This man requires a lot of looking after and intervening for. I must hold the shield over him, the schirm, the breastplate, the lorica, the umbrella. He needs protection, though he doesn't deserve it. The Hand from Heaven that is visible over him is a meteorological manipulation paid for with gold. But there is a genuine and invisible Hand from Heaven pointing to him, and the cloudy subscript of it says, 'Protect this least of mine.' The subscript is written for me. I wish it were for somebody else. I never wanted the job."

"It's your talk that is cloudy, lad," Polder said sourly. "What is your name?"

"Oak."

"Yes? Like the tree?"

"Like the oak tree, like the Og tree, like the tree that was the pole ridge, for it's there that I get my name. Like the roof ridge, perhaps the roof ridge of a sluggish-riding old boat."

"And your family name?" Polder asked.

"Scath," the lad said. But Polder didn't recognize it.

Polder Dossman had all the gestures for a cult figure. They were studied, they were sweeping, they were grand. The way he raised his head like a full-maned but still young lion, the way he compassed a whole world with that comprehensive and hunting look, the way he spread his dripping hands— these were gestures that few could withstand. And lately he had adopted the Hand from Heaven gesture, the pointing outward and downward that was both a legacy and a blessing. Polder, by the regal tossing of his head, gave the impression of incredible strength and swiftness and strategy. He looked to be the man who had no fear in him at all.

"Paper camel! Paper camel!" children were calling at him now. How did they know that his totem animal was the camel? And what did they mean by calling him paper?

"Hot-air camel! Hot-air camel!" they called at him. Well, he would have to have some of those children killed as an example, though he hated to do that in his first week on a world.

"Paint-picture camel! Paint-picture camel!" the kids were gibing at him. He would have those kids done away with quickly enough; but perhaps he could charm their elders to avoid exterminating many of them also. He did have charm, and he began to spread it about in the world.

The way Polder spoke, with that far-carrying power in his voice, with the softness and confidence of edged steel sheathed in velvet, both stunned and soothed his listeners. The central bronze tone and the whispering edges of it shook the very earth with their harmonics; they set small animals and small people to tumbling out of their burrows and dens and strong houses. Polder trumpeted with his rich call, and all the walls fell down before him.

"Pasteboard pig! Ballyhoo boar!" the damnable young of the damnable local humans were bantering. How did they know that the boar had become his secondary totem animal? How did they know that Adonis had become his secondary totem person? And what could they have against such holy things as paper (the first and still the best of the miracle communicators), against such things as hot air (electronic ether), against such things as paint-picture or visual portrayal? In one legendary, man had been made out of the slime of the earth. But now men, and especially transcending men, were made out of winged words, out of contrived and multidimensional portraits, out of the dripping charisma of the gifted, and out of the emotional miasma that floats just above the many-monstered interior ocean. But had not Polder himself now become a monster (a *monstrum*, a showpiece) in that interior ocean? Was he not an archetypical manifestation? He was on the *inside* of the head of every person on every world; he was there in his own person.

Polder's long and fair hair billowed and flowed even when the air moved not at all. This was by special dispensation or arrangement. His eyebrows were like bushy gold fire over the blue fire-ice of his eyes, and they were gently hypnotic in their effect. His slanting grin was like primordial cliffs, and it made his fat jaw line seem indomitable rather than hoggish. His dispensing hands scattered manna and fishhooks, and the latter hooked into the finny vulnerability of every person who encountered him.

"Humpbacked Hog-Nog!" the kids hooted at Polder. "Hog and Og, they raise a fog!"

Polder caught and killed one of the children. The rest fell silent and looked at him with fang-bared hatred. There is no accounting for the responses of children. But he would win even them; he would win everyone to him. He would compel everyone to love and support him. He activated the Hand from Heaven again and let it point down on him.

"I don't like that note on the pointing finger," Polder said. "How much more would the manifestation cost if that little bit of advertising were left off, Moira?"

The note on the pointing finger of the Hand from Heaven read "Sky-Signs and Prodigies by Multi-Media Productions. Call us!"

Moira told Polder what the additional cost would be.

"No, it's too much," he said. "We'll leave it like it is. Many persons, looking at it with only their bare eyes, will hardly notice the note that is written there."

Had Polder Dossman had no intelligence at all behind the finely sculptured flesh and the carefully arched bone of his brow, he would still have won devotees as fast as he could process and indoctrinate them. And there were those who said that Polder did not have any intelligence, who said that his brains had all been gobbled up or spilled out in an encounter in a narrow passage, who said that his seeming intelligence was only the echo and shadow of other intelligences that had flourished in other brains and persons, in projecting minds and personalities. They said that his whole person was only the echo and shadow of other persons in times past and in places apart. And yet those who said these things were often among the most avid followers of Polder; theirs *were* the projecting minds and personalities. Then why did they project them into so dudgery a skull as that of Polder Dossman?

If Polder had possessed no strength or power that he could bring to bear, his appearance of having these things would be as effective as his really having them. If he had been destitute of wealth (in this particular instance he was nearly destitute of it; on his arrival at the world of record he had no more than a dozen kilograms of gold to serve as a picture of what wealth sometimes looked like), he still could have sold his tongue ten thousand times over for whatever wealth was needed, and still have had his first tongue remaining to him with all its eloquence.

If the words he spoke didn't really make sense (and often they did not), the itching ears of his eager listeners would lend the words whatever sense was needed. Such ringing declarations as were his, such contained thunder, such haunting affirmation, such striking and prophetic-sounding parallels—they *could not be* mere gibberish. There is a firm law somewhere that promulgates that such things create their own reason and direction.

"Hog and Og, that's what the hooter kids were bantering," Polder said to the young man Oak Scath. "Did they mean the two of us? Are Og and Oak the same?"

"Oak, Og, yes," the young man said. "I am ancient Og who

rode the ridgepole of the ark all through the deluge, and who held the umbrella over the ark. It was so poorly caulked topside that it would have taken on enough water to sink it otherwise. So will your own craft ship too much water if someone does not hold the umbrella over it, Polder."

"Take care of it, man, take care of it," Polder said. "I'll not be bothered with such details, and I'll not tolerate the devious rains falling on my head."

If Polder had had no sense of commerce and no nose for trends and high-pay discrepancies, he still would have had resounding success at commercial affairs. This was because of the impression he made on people. He was the all-powerful figure who nevertheless needed shielding and guarding. He was the all-wealthy figure to whom it was necessary incessantly to make gifts: of crass money, or of less crass opportunity for money; of auriferous information; of organizational aptitudes and of favorable commercial climates and of lucky trade winds; of cartels; and of multiworld rake-offs. How could Polder have felt uneasy about accepting gifts when they were given with such obvious joy, with such obviously induced joy?

So Polder Dossman was into many profitable businesses from the day of his arrival on that current world. It was as if these things were handled elsewhere by others, and the bountiful decisions were being made in minds other than his own. His own mind had become a narrow and straited area of sterile rocks by this time, or perhaps it was a clutter of broken shards. Young Oak said that it was a mind filled with broken bats of baked-clay bricks, and that these bricks and bats of bricks bore old and entitled writing (Oak saw the writing) that would give document and title to almost any claim Polder might want to make. It's good to have a cluttered mind when it all comes out rich.

But the cultish affairs did not go as well as the commercial affairs. Moira tried, with brochures and songfests and talk-a-

lots, to create Polder's image as that of the "Laughing God."
This remained a failure. Polder was never a good laugher. He
was too jerky, too affected. Perhaps he had been better at it
in former times.

So it happened that, within nine days of Polder's arrival on
the ragged hillside, his commerces were shooting up like
cockleburs in the springtime. But his cult had not yet caught
flame on that world. The cult grotto had very few visitors.
There was an obstacle here.

"Why doesn't my cult thrive, Oak?" Polder asked that
young man. "I'm sure it has thrived in other places in times
past, though my memory is not permitted to tell me where
and when this happened. This world, this aspect here, does
not seem to have a really active cult of any kind. There is a
vacuum for me to fill. I'm sure, from other evidence of art
and high story, that this world has an appreciation for the
heroic and its flavor. Then why does my cult languish, Oak?"

"I don't quite know, Mr. Dossman. Maybe it's just that the
whole idea isn't funny enough."

"Funny? Cults aren't supposed to be funny, Oak. Pleasant,
yes. Gracious, yes. Attractive, yes. Exciting, heart-seizing,
elevating, enfolding, comprehensive, shining, shattering, yes;
but not funny."

"On this world, they had better be funny, Mr. Dossman, or
they had better not be at all," Oak said.

"We will see about that, young man." Polder didn't like to
be contradicted in his views, not by persons, not by worlds.
He believed that he knew about cults and what made them
go. If a cult that was built to his specifications should miss
success in a place, then the fault must be with the place and
not with the cult. And yet he was quite able to change his
specifications for a cult.

"Would it help if I became a Lord of the Zodiac, Oak?"
Polder asked his young assistant and protector.

"*Could* you become a Zodiac Lord? Could you swing it?"

"I think so. I believe I'm entitled to one of the twelve positions. I may make a grab for two. Both the camel and the boar were once in the zodiac. They were defeated in ancient feud, but they still have rights to those places. I want to become a double Lord of the Zodiac in the reconstituted signs of the camel and the boar."

"Well, it can't hurt anything to try it, Mr. Dossman."

"I want you to work very closely with Moira in promoting my cult," Polder told Oak or Og. "In working on this project, we may discover what is wrong with you in respect to the cult. And in this, I believe, what is wrong with you is also what is wrong with the world. We will find out what is wrong with you. We will correct you. And we will correct this world. It's simple."

"No, it isn't simple. But I am," the young man Oak or Og said. "I'm too simple to fall for so compounded a thing as this cult. There are too many moving parts to it. I don't like it; not if it's supposed to be serious, I don't. I will not promote it. I will not work with it at all."

"You will do what I tell you to do," Polder ordered.

"Only if it seems like a good idea," Og Scath said. "Up to now, everything else you've suggested has been a good idea. But your cult isn't. The only thing of yours that I am promoting is Amalgamated Camel Enterprises."

"Very well," Polder said. He knew now what was the matter with Og about the cult. Og was stubborn. But the cult could not tolerate any outside stubbornness. And being stubborn was also what was the matter with that world on that subject. Stubbornness can be cured, but the curing requires certain strategic destructions.

"You are a puzzler, young man," Polder told Oak. "It's as though I remembered you when you were much older. And I'm sure we've had previous encounters before my coming here."

"I had been made responsible for you before you came

here, yes. I was told to wait for you and to watch over you. But I don't remember any earlier encounter between us."

"Responsible for me? Who made you responsible for me, lad?" Polder demanded.

"I'll not tell you who it was. I am not absolutely certain myself of it."

"Responsible for me? Yes, that arrogance was in you at our meeting before this one. And before that, and before that, and before that. But is Dunlunk's Fifth Law enough to account for my almost remembering you?"

"No. I believe it's an older law," Og said. "I don't know how the law is phrased. I really don't know much about it." Og Scath looked at Polder Dossman with puzzled eyes. Scenes flicked past those puzzled eyes and were reflected in them. They were off-this-world scenes, out-of-mind scenes, out-of-context scenes. They were deep and enduring scenes that had happened far away and long ago. And, really, they were scenes that had happened to at least two other persons; but they hadn't happened to Polder Dossman or to Og Scath at all.

How could distant and unremembered acquaintances and friendships among other men have such reflection and near recollection in these two? Well, such things as had happened to alternate or parallel persons had very nearly happened to these two also. That was the only explanation.

"This man Polder is allied with the Eidetic Lords," Og Scath said to Moira and Jake one day, "and with all the various Media Lords. I suppose they have really created him, since he seems to be of doubtful flesh, since all the valid elements of him are clearly artificial. Shall I blame his evil on the Eidetic Lords, then? I must blame it on someone, since I am charged with delivering him from all evil. And the Eidetic Lords who make these things so irresponsibly (for Polder Dossman is a made-thing of theirs) are the true Lords of unreason and darkness. How did such a group and such a situation ever come about?"

"Polder Dossman is such a good man," Moira said, "that I would change every name of everything else in the worlds rather than say that he was anything else than good. I will say that white is black. I will say that sweet is sour. I will say that up is down. And I will say that Polder is a good man. The evidence, of course, is entirely against this. What we need to do is convince the Lord of the Worlds of the fact that Polder is good. But how will the estranged ones like ourselves even get an audience with the Lord of the Worlds?"

Polder was at Oak Scath's place one morning. It was a large and spacious place for so young a man to own, and there were certain things to be found there that were large beyond all reason. There was, for instance, the "bed" of Og Scath. It was on that "bed" that the two men sat.

Well, call it a sofa, then, or a divan. Call it what you will. But a ladder is not required to ascend to most sofas, or to most beds. And most such furnitures are not more than fifteen feet or five meters long, nor more than six feet or two meters wide. It was a very large iron "bed." It seemed to be old. And it was probably of value.

"Oak!" Polder spoke with a twinkle that had once been an eidetic affectation but now had become almost normal, a good-humored, bantering way of talking. "Once you were a much older man. We know that. But I also guess that you were once a very much larger man. And you slept in this giant's bed."

"I still sleep in it, Mr. Dossman," Scath said. "Why should I use another bed when I have this?"

"And, Oak, your coat of arms there on the wall is also giant-sized. It's a coat of arms of an Irish giant family."

"No. We're primordials. We were the only people when I began, and I am still of that only-one people."

"But your coat of arms gives the name of O'Basham. Were your ancestors named that?"

"No, merchant Polder, cult figure Polder, I'm the only one who was titled that. I come from Basham, but I can't locate it in modern geography."

"And what's the central image on the coat, Oak? It looks like a very large covered boat, almost like the ark. Is it?"

"Yes, the ark. Employer Polder, I've told all this to you before, but your mind would not accept or remember it. Nor will it accept or remember it this time. Yes, the ark; the only boat ever built quite like that. It wasn't a successful design, except for one unusual purpose. The strain on it of being masted would have broken it like an eggshell, so it had no masts at all. It was too steep and closed to have oarlocks, so it wasn't rowed. The water soon got too deep for it to be punted, so there was no way of controlling it or moving it at all. It was like a wagon without wheels."

"And that appears to be a very large man sitting astride the roof ridge of that closed and covered ark. The face of that man looks like—"

"It looks like me," Og Scath said.

"Yes. And he's holding what looks very much like a huge umbrella. Why should he sit astride the roof ridge of an open boat out in the rain and hold so big an umbrella as that? He is caught in the rain. That is rain, isn't it?"

"Man, that is rain!" Og swore.

"Why should he sit atop the boat in the rain instead of going inside? Why should he hold that big umbrella? And why should he hold it aside and not over his head?"

"I was holding the umbrella over the main hatch, Mr. Dossman. The hatch would have filled and the boat would have foundered if I hadn't held an umbrella over it."

"Why wasn't the hatch cover on?"

"There wasn't any hatch cover. There was only the great central hatch, and no provisions had been made to cover it.

There was no ventilation at all except for the hatches. The boat and its live cargo would have stifled if the hatches had been on. The design and planning were bad. The designer made a mistake, but I sure will not complain to *him* about it. Why isn't your own hatch cover on, Polder?"

"Oh, I have my own cargo of animals, Oak, and I'm not a very well-ventilated man. You have to admit that your ancestor looks mighty silly sitting straddling that roof ridge and holding a huge umbrella over a boat hatch."

"That is no ancestor. You don't listen. That is myself."

"What? You? Not really. I do believe it's an ancestor. I always say, Oak, that an alternate or parallel of one's own person is only an ingrown ancestor. Our ancestors can be divided off from our persons by more things than time."

"It is myself and no ancestor. Would I remember such a thing if I hadn't been there?"

"How is it painted, Oak? Or how is it done in whatever medium?"

"In water color, Mr. Dossman. In water color and in sky color. Am I an artist? I don't know how it was done. I was there, and this is the imprint of my being there. Have you a coat of arms yourself?"

"I think so," Dossman said uncertainly, "but it isn't completed. There are still several cantons of it that lack devices."

Og Scath drove a thriving business for Polder. A young man who is so good at a business is entitled to a few pretensions and quirks and oddities. But he went too far and stumbled over too much: he had learned a secret.

He had learned that Polder Dossman wasn't real.

And now the same knowledge swept over Polder Dossman like green nausea. He knew himself to be an artificial contrivance, a stuffed sausage of a puppet who had been made by manipulators for a joke. He knew this for an instant, and then he smashed that knowledge in himself into a hundred pieces. Whether he was something, whether he was nothing, he would still pretend to be a god.

My corpse, my core, my nerves, my nous,
Are artificial, gimp and gaster.
But whose the artifice? And who's
The artificial puppet-master?

Anon., *Eidetic Elegies*

Polder Dossman went to see Hector Bogus, who was one of the local Eidolon or Media Lords. Hector had the reputation of being much more technical than most of the Lords.

"You're as pleasant a sight as rain in parched places," Hector said pleasantly, "and as devious as the devil himself. I have heard of your magnetism and charm. I wonder if your magnetism will work on a nonferrous person like myself? But you do make a fine appearance, Polder. And now you have come to tell me my own business, which I know pretty well, and which you do not know at all. Is that not the way it is, Dossman?"

"No, it is not, Bogus. There is nothing whatever of which you can say that I know it not at all. I understand all the media quite well, and I understand the print-out areas in much detail. Wherever I have been, I have always worked very closely with the Eidetic and Media Lords. And then I have my own unnamed medium in which I'm expert. It consists of setting certain modifications into the larger media flow. I am the solar medium in this, and the conventional media are the planetaries to me. The words and messages and gestures are furnished by myself, and the amplifications will be furnished by you working Lords in the field."

"It sounds like a mighty lame arrangement, Dossman. But I'm no Lord of any sort."

"Have your disclaimers if it pleases you. But I know your power, and I want to modify a portion of that power-flow to my own satisfaction and to the bettering of the world. What are you playing with?"

Hector Bogus was taking small effigies or dolls out of a cigar box, giving them a sort of galvanic shock between two brass balls which were opposite members of a condenser, and then setting them down to run about on his desk in a fever of life or pseudolife.

"I like to give them an appearance of animation and let them run around in the huge hippodrome that is the top of my desk," Bogus said. "Ah, Polder, I believe that someone liked to give you the appearance of animation and to let you run in a limited spaciousness. And I believe that this someone is getting tired of watching you run and is about ready to disanimate you and put you back in the box."

"I am no effigy, Bogus. I am real. You may find that out abruptly."

But this man Hector Bogus made Polder nervous. How did

Hector know of Polder's queasy little daydreams or premoni-
tions that he might not be real, that he might be no more
than somebody's animation? Hector Bogus was putting one
of his own little animations into a sort of torture cabinet. He
bellowed small flames into the cabinet then to get a
white-hot fire going. There was a small explosion, and some
wires and transistors burst out of the little creation. Bogus
screwed a jeweler's glass in his eye, repaired the wiring, and
returned the small image to its torture. And it was torture!

"It is fun to manufacture a small person of exquisite and
intense response and appreciation of pain and of time,"
Bogus said. "One can study a soul in hell by this device. The
pain is real to the animation, Polder, and the pain is eternal.
There is no doubt that the image is horribly conscious of the
pain. It does have consciousness; I devised it a consciousness
that consists of an ingenious resonating circuit. Have you an
even more ingenious resonating circuit in yourself, Polder,
and does it serve you as well as a real consciousness? This
little thing I have just put into the torture cabinet, it is living
eternities and eternities of screaming pain in every second. I
built this intense appreciation of time into it. You can barely
hear it, but should I amplify it (and I have done so several
times for fun), it becomes such a loud and horrifying
screaming that it sends people into shock in all this part of
the town. But I have my own amplification turned on. I can
hear him with total intensity."

"You like to do that?" Polder asked as he licked his lips. He
liked the idea of it himself.

"Certainly I like it," Bogus said. "And the beauty is that the
manufacturer and observer (myself), after such pleasures, can
salve his conscience by saying, 'He isn't real.' He isn't. But, to
itself, the pain and the existence are real.

"What, does my little animated hint remind you of
something, Polder? You have suspected that you are manu-

factured? You have suspected that, once someone turns you on fully, you will have the exquisite and intense response to pain and to time? You seem thoughtful, Polder."

"Oh, I was thinking of certain screaming metals used in various instrumentations. They are put under terrific stress by torsion and heat, and they respond with waves at various complex frequencies. To me it sometimes seems that they are screaming in agony."

"Of course they are, Polder, to themselves. But to a neutral observer it is all measurable physical reaction. So, I suspect, is the case with you. You have been worrying about not being real, Polder. Worrying is also a measurable physical reaction. And you begin to worry that this may really be Prime World."

Bogus extinguished the small and hot fire in the toy cabinet. He took the suffering animation out, killed it by dipping it for a moment into a shot glass of corrosive sublimate (thus did the alchemists disanimate their miniatures), and put it back into the cigar box.

"Oh, well, if it's artificial and electrical, then it isn't live," Polder said dully.

"Not necessarily so, Polder," Bogus maintained. "Life *is* artificial. That's one of the characters by which it may be known. And God was personally well into the electronic age by the time of the particular creations. The sophistication of our wiring schematics does not say whether we are live or not. There is very primitive life. You are pretty primitive yourself.

"You're about through, Dossman. You know that, don't you? You're into your last world." Bogus showed just the curling edge of his scorn.

"I'll pay you back for your tedious affronts, Bogus. But are you not maintenance and repair station for Hand from Heaven presentations on this world?"

"No. There isn't any such station here. Yours is the only

Hand from Heaven on this world. And they never need repair or maintenance. I can modify the things slightly if you're interested."

"All right. I want it to *just* have thundered and lightened at the first appearance of the Hand. I want the echo and the afterflash, and the memory, of the thunder and lightning to be still hanging in the air. I want the sun to be sparkling on rain drops so small and attenuated that they are unable to complete their downward fall. Yes, gold sparkle in the air, and the memory of thunder and lightning. And the after-the-rain smell of wet sweet clover and amaranth."

"All right. I can make the modifications in the Hand phenomena. I'll do it. But why did you really come to see me, Dossman?"

"The reason for my visit? I sent certain announcements around to your chain, Bogus, and they weren't published. It was an oversight, I'm sure, but I want it corrected at once. It is important that these announcements be widely published."

"You are referring to your naive advertisements for your own cult, Dossman? Oh, I won't publish such things, and no other responsible publisher will either. It might be better—no, it might be worse if you tried the obscenity presses on this. Some of those shoddies will publish almost anything, if they're paid an unreasonable amount to do it."

"There are *no* presses except the obscenity presses, Bogus. There are no Media publications, whether scatter-ray or focus-ray or ether-tinsel or solid-light transmission, except of the obscenity sort. And there is no art or argument or ethic anywhere except the obscenity variety. Obscenity loosens the tongues of all these things, and without obscenity those tongues would be tied forever. I have the impression that I once knew you or an echo of you some worlds back; you were a much younger man then. Your name was Trenchant, and you were a false Lord Spiritual."

"And your name was Pilgrim, but you were a false Peter Pilgrim, not the true Peter Pilgrim of myth. But, Polder, you know that we're unable to know the names of our corresponding figures on other worlds. It's absolutely impossible that we should have this recognition. And the young mock Lord, Trenchant, he isn't and he certainly wasn't an exact correspondence to me. He hadn't learned cruelty yet. Or disbelief.

"Yes, I was a much younger man then, Dossman. You can leave now."

"Do you not go grand on me, Eidetic Lord, Media Lord, Advocate Lord, Wiggly-Word Lord!" Polder burst out in angry voice. "Get ready, or be left! The water is moving! The tide is running! *I* am the one who is moving it all. Every beach and shingle in every world will be covered with the dead and broken small creatures who waited too long to join the tide. The tide turns now, and it leaves them stranded. Small creature Bogus, easily broken small creature, I am that tide!"

"Tell that to your cultic followers, little pewter god Dossman. Continue to shuffle your commerce if you wish, and you can have a good enough future here. But do not threaten, do not cultify, do not corrupt! But if you disturb, if you distort, if you kill, if you perform any of the abominations that are attributed to you by death's-land account or off-world rumor, then we will break you. And, as a broken one, you will go to the final place forever. There are those of us who have the power to break you, even if we dislike using that power."

"Somewhere, I suppose, there are fish that dislike water," Polder said. "Somewhere there are bees that hate clover. There are kine that dislike green pastures and fresh water; they'd rather eat hot dust and drink ashes. And there are birds that would rather crawl on their bellies than travel in air. There are all of those things somewhere, I know, but I have never seen any of them. Nor have I known Lords of the

Talking-Air, Lords Spiritual, Lords of the Media, Eidetic Lords who do not love to use their power.

"But the fact is, Bogus, that you use your power blindly when you are left to yourselves. Your power must be brought into focus by cultic figures like myself, or figures unlike myself but capable as I am of originating vital movements. All of you must be directed and impelled by a small multitude of such shimmering persons as myself, by such shining folks as are scarcely to be found at all on this local world.

"I notice there is a startling deficiency of cults here. Even the inept cults are missing. This emptiness has to be filled, and mostly it has to be filled by myself. It's a weak world you have here, Bogus, until you can come up to the impelling level of the creative cults."

"No. This is a strong world," Hector Bogus said. "We have the strength and the grace here. We're fortunate in everything. We have discovered the Larger Thing, and we're intimate with it. We know it, whether we live up to it or not. Why, having the Thing Itself, should we lust after a ten-times-removed shadow of it?"

"Bogus, you are raw material and I will regard you that way," Polder said. "I'll chop you and I'll harvest you; and I'll reseed you so that you'll not be extinguished. The Lords of the Media can play any realm or any world like a piano. They can direct a world and all its thought—most often, in all its unthought. They can compel a world absolutely to any notion. They can do these things if numinous persons show them how to do them."

"We know how, Dossman. We can do whatever we want to do, but in many places we've begun to practice restraint. Why should we indulge in sinful abuses of power?"

"Consternation on you, Bogus!" Polder whipped with his flexible voice. "Power is *made* to be abused! That's the whole purpose of it. You Lords of the Imagery and the Effigy can set all the idiots of a world braying like asses. You can set the people-parrots to squawking and squalling. You can make them gibber to each other any message you wish to exploit. First you can move them to noise, then you can move them to action. You can move mountains, if you first set up the compelling opinion that the mountains must be moved. You can do all these things. You can construct and create. There is nothing that cannot be made out of those building bricks of noise and stifling air. If we of the intense elite show you how, there is no limit to what you can effect."

"We learn how to set limits," Bogus said, "and we do not need the brittle elites to show us how to do anything. The strong know how to kill the weak. The intelligent know how to seize advantage from the stupid. The rich understand how the screws might be tightened on the poor. The living know how easy it is to remove the hands and the heritage of the dead. But none of these things is commonly done here. We have been building a harder thing than power: we've been building fences around it. Often we are given the necessary grace to restrain ourselves from the depredations. And, if we carelessly lose or spill some of that grace, then we must humbly beg for more."

"When did any Media Lord ever do any thing humbly? Why do you make these pretenses, you who torture small creations?"

"Oh, I torture the little fabrications of my own so that I won't be torturing the larger fabrications. I do it because I climb out of one pit, only to fall into another. But I keep climbing. This world has acquired quite a number of climbers. And we won't have it set back again. We know what your own cultishness amounts to."

"Bogus, you're a howling hypocrite!" Polder Dossman cried with that far-carrying power in his voice, with the threatening softness and the electrifying confidence of edged steel sheathed in velvet. But Hector Bogus seemed unelectrified by it.

"You're a hypocrite," Polder called in a higher key. *"You have to be!* There's no sense at all to things if people aren't hypocrites. Grace is for those without impetus or power. I swear by every obscenity that the evil will always turn the good over a fire as though on a spit. Ah, the folks of the good nations, we'll roast them whole. We'll even roast their screaming. And they'll come to their own barbecuing under their own power because the Lords of the Media will tell them to come. And the Lords will tell them to come because we of the high elite will tell the Lords."

"Polder Dossman, nobody can be set all the way down on first evidence. Are you evil for certain?"

"Yes, for certain, Bogus. To be evil is to call everything by its right name. My own preying on any world is always the primary action on that world. To cut me out would be like cutting a bowstring to let the bow go slack. A slack bow is no bow at all. It would be like cutting a sinew to relax a limb. Bogus, the worlds were weighty and without movement for a billion billion years. They did not stir. They did not move. And without movement there cannot be any real life. The primordial weight sat like a primordial toad or stone. And the name of this original weight that was without motion and without light was 'The Good.' And then a counterweight introduced itself, and the worlds began to move and to live. And the name of this counterweight has always been 'The Evil.' I am the counterweight newly arrived in this world, and I will compel it to move and to live. There wasn't much movement or life apparent when I got here. Where did you get your name of Bogus?"

"We were living and moving before you came, Polder. If you could not see it, the fault was with your own eyes. I have my name from my father, and he from his. We are called Bogus because we are bogus Lords. It is all for fun, the Lord play, the big-man play; it becomes evil only when it becomes serious. Deliver me from evil! Deliver me from serious evil and from evil seriousness, and fortify me against the intimidating scorn of evil persons! Let me walk in the light and hear the laughter of God."

"That's my thing, Bogus. I've been having my cult promote the title the 'Laughing God' for myself. I discovered that there was a local leaning toward some such name. The notices I sent to your publications, the notices you did not publish, they were very much on the 'Laughing God' theme."

"It didn't work, did it, Dossman? Not for you. You're not capable of real laughter. And you're just not the god type."

"Oh, but I am! I have to be!" Polder cried. His flexible voice cracked where it was supposed to achieve unbroken effect. "I look the part, Bogus. I act the image. I—Bogus, you're laughing at me! I'll not be laughed at! My person is above that!"

"Polder, you are no more than one of the little fabrications to be kept in a cigar box most of the time. Then you are taken out occasionally and set on somebody's desk or sideboard, and you believe you have been born again into a new world. You're a miniature effigy, a badly made one. And to torture you would not be the same thing as torturing something real." Hector Bogus was laughing as he poured it on. He knew that Polder Dossman was not something to be kept in a cigar box. In a bigger box, perhaps.

"Man, I'll destroy you if you don't come around," Polder huffed. "My tide is running now. Join it before it's too late. If you do not—"

"—then you'll designate me to be a dead and broken small creature stranded on the beach when the tide deserts it, will you, Polder? I like my own cigar box analogy better, and I like you as the miniature much better. Be careful, Polder, even on your imagined beach. I'm a crawfish! I can slide sideways and backward to backwaters if need be. Your tide has run out; that's all it is. I'm not like to be broken or to perish on a backwater beach.

"I have my own tide, Polder, and it's rising in me now. I have heard it told that you are a man of great strength and agility, both physically and mentally. I have heard this told, and I'm almost certain it was you who told it. Let's try it, then. You will go out from here quickly and quietly, or I will throw you out quickly and not quietly. There's no other choice for you, and you haven't enough strength or ability to create one. But stay here another minute if you want to be broken by my own tide on my own sand."

"No, man, no," Polder Dossman said slowly and hedgingly. "There will be another day very soon, and I will have cut all your own sand from under you when it comes."

Polder went out to leave Hector Bogus, who was a mock Lord of the Eidetics and Media. But Bogus followed him out. Polder's Hand from Heaven was hovering low there where Bogus had had it pulled down for modification.

And Bogus suddenly, roguishly, rather boyishly, set some special modifications into the Hand. Look out for it! It's big; it's impulsive with a high-sky charisma; it has, from its associations, a cloud-capping humor; it's mindless, but it has intuition that is otherwise based; and it partakes of the almighty.

The great Hand came down, took Polder by the scruff and the crine, and lifted and swooped with him for a hundred meters. There it dipped him into a vat of corrosive sublimate that a processor had in his reduction yard for breaking up discarded lumps of flesh and bones. The Hand held Polder in the vat for a moment (till he was dead), then lifted him further and deposited him in an ash-box in a trash area.

Oh, but this impulsive action by Hector Bogus, by the Hand from Heaven, by the whole cooperating neighborhood of little industrial back yards, brought quick and loud response from several concerned and entrapped persons! The young man Og Scath was there instantly.

"Thrones and Powers!" Og howled as he came at a run to a

site. "Bogus, you've gone too far. You've killed him! He was one of the protected ones. You should have known that. You're a master of eidetics. You know when an effigy is protected!"

"No, I didn't; I sure didn't. Why should a thing so worthless be protected? Oh, the gruesome humor of God! Why are these reservations placed against every honest impulse? Well, I've got to fix it then, I guess."

"That was unethical to have him seized by his own Hand that he had contracted for and possibly paid for," Moira Mara complained. "Oh, he's dead. I'll be held partly responsible. I think I've already been held responsible for it before. What can be done? He's dead, I tell you, Bogus. You've killed him."

"Oh, maybe not. He wasn't really alive. He had left off being alive, left off being a man a long time ago. Someone filled him with the god-goop long ago, and he believed in himself. But those things are always done for utilitarian purpose. The peasants on that side are supposed to believe; we on the manipulation side may not believe in our own galopading goop. The run-amuck ones have always been a trouble. And Og tells me now that the Polder was 'protected.' Well, I understand the small animations, and he isn't any more intricate. A touch of the galvanic shock and we'll have him fixed as bad as ever."

Bogus set further special modifications into the dangling control of the Hand. The Hand came down again, caught Polder up, and moved him to a shock-plastic yard. It lifted him in between two very large brass balls that were opposite members of a giant condenser. The operator of the shock-plastic manufacturing company built up the voltage on the condenser, up and up to the flash point. It flashed.

And Polder Dossman twitched with apparent life.

"Real life cannot be restored by galvanic shock," Jake Mara protested fretfully.

"No. But eidetic life can be," Bogus said, "which is proof positive of what we are dealing with."

For Polder Dossman was alive. Whether his was only a Media-created, eidetic life or whether it was a real life is something that will have to be argued out between the eidetics and the reals. The Hand from Heaven set Polder down on his feet and patted him on the head.

"The thirst, the thirst, the terrible thirst!" Polder croaked with thickened tongue as he clasped his own throat.

"You're wrong, Bogus," Og Scath exclaimed. "His life *is* real. Eidetic contrivances do not suffer resurrection thirst on being reanimated."

"No, of course they don't. But sometimes they think they do. They mimic living forms in both mental and physical processes."

Water, green camel milk, and whey were brought to Polder Dossman. He drank nervously and noisily. He shuddered and moaned and drank some more.

"Now you will just get busy and make it up to him, Bogus!" Moira was saying hotly. "You will modify that Hand to give him every benefice we can imagine, or we'll have you for illegal tampering."

"Aye, you have me where I'm short, young lady," Hector Bogus said. "I'll do what I can. That's the only Hand on this world, so I don't know much about them."

"You're the only one who knows anything about them. Now then, we want low, rumbling thunder about him all the time," Moira said, "and we want it to conform to this beat." She gave Bogus a notation or score. "It's our cult tune or chant. And lightning should be flickering around him constantly. Not just any little lightning; we want sky-high stuff."

"Aye, we'll make a hot Hand of it all," Bogus said glumly. Polder Dossman looked mighty disheveled and sick. "It's grotesque when an experimental contrivance like Polder goes out of control and becomes a cult figure," Bogus complained. "Ah, why do even the people of no brains at all follow such a fellow?"

"And Resurrection Roses, the towering aroma of them—" Moira was enumerating.

A tidal wave, a forest fire
So hot and strong that nothing caps it,
A juggernaut, a gobbling pyre;
What power ventures to collapse it?

S. Smith, *Cup to Lip Compendium*

"Ovations, Triumphs, Exultations, Accolades, Fanfares, Flourishes, let them all pour out! Let the days be scandalous with loud light and the nights be sleepless with shouting! Let it be the millennium, the thousand years, or the thousand days! As if there were a difference!" Moira Mara was giving the orders for the thing, and Hector Bogus was making halfhearted notes.

"That's enough," Bogus said. "However did I become eidolon-chief on this scurvy little world? We'll give Polder a

194

little noise for his cult, and a little sky-pageant. But we won't overdo it."

"That is not enough!" Moira whooped. "Of course we'll overdo it. We want spectacles, prodigies, monstrals, miraculi. We want everything."

"It will look better for everyone if Polder thrives," the young-old man Og said. You eidolon creators, Bogus, you Media manipulators, you don't want a failure hung around your necks."

"What matter. We've had many. And I believe that this Polder person has had many failures in other places. There may be human correspondences to Media creations, and I believe that this Polder is one. Many of the eidolon creatures in fact were originally human, and the Media superstructure was grafted onto the human person. And some humans had, from the very first, an orientation similar to those of Media contrivances. I suppose he's flesh basically. But I wonder if he may not be partly of what is called cryptically 'hump-backed flesh,' that plastic, less-than-human substratum that gives us so much trouble. We don't understand it really, and intuition is useless when one runs into the amorphous stuff. We're going to destroy him. I wish it would be fun to destroy him, but it's only fun to destroy a good person. Notice that sometime. Polder must be someone's experimental model. We'll have to find what has gone wrong with the experiment and make a report to the experimenter on whatever world he operates. I will get a writ and have Doctor Hans August and some of his associates examine him." Bogus seemed worlds-weary and exasperated.

"No, no, those doctors take one apart to examine one," Jake Mara protested.

Polder had begun to speak, loudly and eloquently, but it was in a language that none present could understand.

"Oh, certainly, Polder will have to be disassembled,"

Hector Bogus said. "He's of no interest the way he is, but a minute investigation of his parts might reveal something. These persons of eidolon construction erected on a human base are pretty unstable. They world-jump a lot, for one thing. I've protested against such manufacturing. But we simply do not get really fine physical detail in completely artificial persons. And the human base should work all right, if we scrape it clean, if we assure that it will be no more than a base. I have preached to my colleagues here and on other worlds: 'Be sure there's no live spark left in one. Just one live spark can flame the most awkward tinder, and then we are left with an unpleasant and stenchy conflagration that walks and talks like a man. We should always terminate one that gets the "walk-abouts" and goes wrong.' But many of my colleagues are themselves back-feed constructs of eidolon and human."

Polder was declaiming with wonderful power. None of those present could understand his words, but all of them understood his power a little.

"It's like the old sculptor who carved a statue of a sculptor complete with chisel and mallet," Bogus said. "And the original sculptor put a bit too much of himself into the sculptor-statue. So that statue in turn carved a statue more sophisticated than himself. And that second statue carved a third, and so it went till there were nine of the statues or eidolons variously made. And the nine eidolons had progressed from the plain stone of the first one to the rapture-flesh of the ninth. Then they all turned on the old sculptor himself and began to unlimb him for his improvement. I tell you that won't work. The basic human sculptor would be justified in obtaining writs for the disassembly and destruction of the nine images. And we are justified in getting a writ for the destruction of Polder Dossman."

Polder was speaking powerfully and movingly, but without literal meaning.

"Fix his voice and expression," Moira told Bogus. "The tone is fine and spirited and a little bit ghostly. But it isn't making sense. Put some sense into it."

"I'm not doing it," Bogus protested. "I hadn't even begun to work on his voice or expression. That's coming to him from somewhere else."

"I tell you, you are *not* justified in destroying Polder," Jake Mara said harshly. "Better to destroy a hundred worlds than one such spirit as this. How would there be improvement if the first flesh should carry veto power over its superior derivatives?" That was more than Jake Mara usually spoke.

But now all of them, even Hector Bogus, had become a little afraid of the power in Polder's voice and person. There was nothing quite like that fiery eloquence in the unknown tongues. Even Bogus, who was supplying part of the effect, the tongues of fire that flicked in and out of the mouth of Polder, was impressed.

"He is genuine," Og said. "He has become one of the archetypes in the ocean that underlies every mind. He has become one of the Lords of the Zodiac. This is greatness."

"No," Bogus objected, though he was becoming uncertain on the matter, "it isn't genuineness; it isn't greatness. It's just the way the dice roll. Oh, little green eidolon-godlings! I just thought of something. What if he achieves highest and least known status of all? What if he becomes one of the seven Dice Throwers? There's a vacancy, you know. Merope has disappeared to most of the worlds for near a decade now."

"But Merope, one of the Seven Sisters of the Pleiades, is female."

"Not necessarily; not always," Og said. "Within my own type-memory, Merope has been seven times female, seven times hermaphrodite, and six times male."

"It would be odd if Merope were back in the sky tonight," Jake Mara said.

"Odd. It would be disastrous!" Hector Bogus exploded.

"This misbegotten freak, and you his twitter-brained followers, have gotten clear out of hand."

Merope was back in the sky that night. Would she, he, have a hot hand for the dice? Would he throw them well for himself?

"It does not really matter whether Polder has become one of the High Seven Dice Throwers," Moira said. "But it must be believed that he has become one of the seven. I suspect, with the treasonable part of my mind, that he has not become either Archetype or Zodiac Lord. But it must be believed that he is these things; and I myself will believe it all with the more faithful parts of my brains."

And from that night on till the end of it, the cult movement was like a skyrocket. A skyrocket is a meteor that falls upward and is not consumed. The cult grew by the hundreds, by the thousands, by the millions, even. Every person who signed with the cult signed with a pen that writhed with cold, phosphorescent fire; but the new joiners believed that it was only their intense faith that kept them from being burned. And each new cult person received a tongue of fire that hovered over his head night and day and followed wherever he went.

Polder spoke and blessed and cursed and withered and healed mostly in high gibberish in those days. But now and then he talked to Moira and Jake and Og Scath in almost rational speech out of a corner of his mouth.

Polder sent a command to every ruler in that world to abdicate on a certain very near day. The cult, by intuitive accord and implementation, would take care of all the affairs of the world, Polder said. The abdication commands were also sent to all subrulers, province heads, county heads, business executives, bureaucrats, high and middle and low officials, and tacit leaders—about a million persons in all.

These commands were sent out with individual handling and detailing, and all in the same day.

That would take a large work force, would it not? No. No more than three or four persons were employed in the work. Intuitive Implementation really does work, to a degree. It takes the place of all addressographs and labeling machines, all gang-print machines, all mailing and dispatching. The messages were simply intuited to take form and to arrive in the proper time at the proper place.

Some persons were puzzled at receiving their abdication commands; some were angry; some were frightened. But none of the persons on that world was puzzled as to the identity of the flaming cult figure Polder Dossman. The intuition of Polder's personality was the strongest thing going out.

Then Polder sent out twelve billions of sets of abdication commands to twelve billion worlds. The Intuitive Implementation was not quite so strong here, and the delivered messages were often a bit hazy. Was Polder biting off too much? Possibly. Not everyone on the twelve billion worlds intuited Polder's personality. Here and there the messages encountered absolute incomprehension.

But on his operating world, on his world of record, Polder began to hold very large meetings in the evenings. There were impossible circumstances connected to these gatherings, but the impossibilities seemed to be easily solved. It would seem rather improbable that a million persons could gather on a plot no more than a hundred meters on a side, and that each of these persons could be speaking to Polder Dossman at once, could be understood by him, and could understand him also, though he still spoke the convoluted high gibberish.

There was a little resentment developing against this gibberish, and it irrupted into abrasive heckling. And the abrasive heckling quickly irrupted into a number of twitching corpses.

But Polder performed massively. He received huge gifts; he spread out his beneficent hands; he thundered and lightened with casual movements of those beneficent hands; he blessed, and sometimes he cursed; he blew minds; he left cooling corpses twitching on the ground; he withered; and he healed.

There was fear and trembling, there was lamentation, and there was high hope; there were the real goods certified and delivered. But was it possible that some fragment of humor had appeared in that cloud-wrapped, thunder and lightning eidolon-man at whom the mile-long finger of the Hand from Heaven pointed morning and night? Humor in Polder? Well, here was a person in great pain from a rotted and abscessed tooth and begging to be cured. And Polder did cure him of his pain and his poisoning. But did he restore the tooth to its original sound state, white and healthy and unblemished? No, not quite. He lanced and healed and drilled and filled that tooth, but he did not fill it with its own original substance; he filled it with a bogus-gold plug. And the plug even bore the stamp "Plugs by Suggs." Suggs was a local dental supply and plug house. The creatures of every eschatological case laughed at that one.

But Polder was startled by the laughter. "Find out why they're laughing, Moira." He spoke out of the side of his mouth to Moira Mara.

"They're laughing because it was funny," she said.

"Oh," he grunted, and then he went into high gibberish again. But he still didn't understand the laughing. Shouldn't an Archetype and a Zodiac Lord and a High Dicer even understand his own joke?

There were millions of healings though, hundreds of thousands of witherings, tens of thousands of simple blessings, a few hundred twitching corpses of hecklers and heathens. The heckler movement had lost momentum from so many of its practitioners being turned into twitching corpses. There had been those who guessed that the hecklers might abandon their tactic. They didn't, though.

For now there came a night meeting when the hecklers were stronger and louder and more bitter than they had ever been before. And they were better armed against the strike-dead tactic. Who had armed them against it, and how? This was the eve of the great abdication and take over day, and a feeling of powerful confrontation had been building up. There had even been threats that the cult might be defied. But the hecklers tonight did not seem to be of the ruling or official consensus. They seemed to be young and informed and determined and vengeful. Whatever could they be vengeful about?

Polder watched it building up. He began to talk out of the side of his mouth to his closest people, not in high gibberish though, but in rational if somewhat nervous speech.

"I am an Archetype," he whispered melodiously in one of his golden asides. "I am a Zodiac Lord. I am one of the High Dice Throwers, and our dicing is another name for Fate. How can anything be happening that I do not know about? How can there be meanings hidden from me?"

"Tin tongue, tin tongue. Empty barrel, broken bung," some of the hecklers were chanting. How could they be so metallurgically ignorant? Polder was always known as the golden tongue, not as the tin tongue.

"We don't understand it either," Moira said. "Can't you kill them?"

"I'll try it again," the baffled Polder pledged. He killed several persons in the throng with his lightning. Afterward he tried it on the hecklers. But his lightning shattered on whatever shield they were using. The lightning blew back; it exploded; it rained fire on everyone except the hecklers.

Polder attacked the hecklers electrically. But they were electrically shielded.

Polder attacked them meteorologically, with whirlwind and plasma explosion. And they were meteorologically shielded.

"Find out what you can about them, Jake," Polder whispered furiously. "It's important."

"A challenge, a challenge," one of the hecklers was crying in a ringing voice. "Gibberish is no sign of power. Gibberish can be faked, and you fake it. But there is a test of power and faith that cannot be faked."

"Is Bogus crossing me?" Polder whispered angrily.

"He says he isn't," Moira answered. "And some of the assaults you throw are his. But some are your own devices. The failures are your own."

"Yes, that's true," Polder said. He healed three persons absentmindedly, and then he blasted one person dead. Change of pace—that's always been the thing. Heal them all, and they will no longer come to you in fear and trembling. But why was he not able to blast the hecklers tonight?

Polder attacked the hecklers encaustically. He burned to death a few persons who were standing near some of the groups of hecklers, but he could not burn the hecklers. They were shielded encaustically.

"The hecklers are angry because you have killed the children of some of them," Jake Mara said as he arrived back with the hasty information. "There are some of these people who consider the killing of their children as an insult. To them it's as serious a thing as trampling their gardens or hewing down their trees."

"A challenge, a challenge!" many of the hecklers were chanting. "We challenge you to a display of power." They made an increased noise about it, and one could not quite see what they were up to.

"What do I do?" Polder asked in a whisper.

"Accept their challenge," Og Scath answered. "I am your shield and your protection and I tell you this. This shield-man tells you that it is sometimes a good idea to lower the shield and come out to unrehearsed meeting. You have more imagination than any group of hecklers, and you have infinitely more power. Anything they can imagine for a challenge, you can do it, or you can seem to do it. Rise to your heights, Polder. You haven't really risen to your heights for several evenings now."

Polder Dossman, eidolon-man and cult figure, Archetype and Zodiac Lord, member of the High Seven Dicers who are the same as Fate, rose to his heights.

There was the curling and pleasant mockery on his mouth. There was the unbroken-horse look in his eyes. There was the incredible vulgarity in the set of his fat jaw. He was the handsome man with the contoured and flowing fair hair; with the powerful and carrying voice, whether for reason or for gibberish. He was the man with the shimmer, with the dazzle about him. He was the hypnotic man, the electric man, the magnetic man, the transcendent man. He was the man with the magic hands that dripped light, that dripped grace and gift, that dripped seed and solace, that dripped healing. That dripped death. The spreading out of his hands was always a grand gesture. And his intricate and carrying voice was always power itself.

"I accept your challenge!" Polder cried, not in golden gibberish, but in a voice of message. "Name it. Tell it. Set it out. There is nothing you can imagine that I cannot do. If I fail in any test, then I step down and put off my attributes. Then you can break me to pieces and grind me like grain. Speak up! I challenge your challenge."

"You are a faker. Gibberish is easily faked," a lead heckler was bawling. "You pretended athletes of the special gifts and graces, the proof that you give of your specialness is no proof at all. You flaunt the gift of tongues, that last refuge of a scoundrel. You say that yours are tongues of fire, but it is fake fire. There is one proof you cannot fake."

"Tell me the unfakable proof and I will prove myself by it," Polder said with that voice that made everything seem momentous. "Anything you can imagine, I can do."

"Snake handling can be faked," another heckler took it up. "Speaking in tongues is the fakery beyond any other. Poison drinking can be faked. Even loving one's neighbor can be faked. But there is one proof that will convince."

"Name it," said Polder with golden patience. He cracked lightning around them like bullwhips, but it was only fun-lightning.

"Mountain-moving!" a thousand hecklers barked together. There was a long pause as the shaft went home to Polder.

"There's no way to fake that, is there?" Polder whispered to his nearest followers.

"No, there sure isn't," Og Scath admitted, "and my advice was wrong. I try to hold the umbrella over you and your doings, but I find that my protecting umbrella has a hole in it big enough for a mountain to pass through."

"It's better this way," Polder said with a sort of nervous glow. "I'd never have tried it except for the hecklers. I'd always have been in doubt about one of my own powers, except for this testing."

"There isn't any way, Polder." Hector Bogus spoke as he came to Polder's side. "I'd know it if there were. I've been forced to take you as a client, and I've done all I could. But there just isn't any way to move a mountain."

"Yes. There is one way," Polder said softly.

"Leave off conferring with your prop men and your dogs and your ariels and your umbrella peddlers, Polder Dossman," the head heckler was bawling out. "You have your challenge. If your cult is the true one, if all authority in the worlds should abdicate to you, then answer the challenge and give proof. Move a mountain and we will believe that you have faith and power sufficient. There, above our town, looms the mountain named Shining Mountain. Move it! Why are you silent? Why do you not speak? Or act?"

"Be quiet." Polder spoke softly but carryingly in his powerful and intricate voice. His right hand was raised in a gesture of power. In his left hand he held an attribute, a camel goad. "Watch the mountain," he said.

The mountain moved.

Any description of mountain-moving is understatement. It can't be helped. It wasn't illusion. Nor was it some tricky weightlessness. The mountain rose and moved in its full weight and mass. There was earthquake, there was airquake, there was skyquake. There was a blast of heat; there was a fearful scurry of clouds and the rising of high towers of dust and hot vapor. There was a dazzling gushing of decapitated fountains. There was unnatural lightning discharge between the dangling roots of the mountain and the raucous pit they had left.

There was a roaring of boulders and the riving wail of split slate strata. The long igneous roots of the mountain broke, turning from thin threads to thousand-ton fragments. Hot fires quickly scorched the mountain itself, and its pine trees flamed and crowned. Deer and goats leaped from the mountain and posed in graceful swift fall against the writhing clouds, picked out by the lightning that now suffused the whole night sky.

The mountain moved swiftly. It stood over the area of the gathering. Looking up at it, one might see flames and explosions working through the whole shaggy underside of the mass. Seven large clusters of boulders fell and killed the seven main groups of hecklers. Then the mountain moved off south and east. Its swift progress could be followed for more than an hour by its roaring and by the unnatural lightning that hovered above it.

The mountain-moving incident had marked Polder Doss-man's highest height. From there on he went down rapidly. And at once.

The Hand from Heaven that had pointed out Polder for these last several weeks had been destroyed by the mountain-moving. Outrageous rains began to fall on the gathering area about an hour after the mountain-moving. The people had stood silent and stunned for that hour. Then the sudden drenching and dangerous flooding broke up the gathering, the last gathering that the Polder Dossman cult would ever hold. Why would it be the last?

Had not Polder given proof of his power? He had. But now there came a reaction to that proof. Mountain-moving will always set up an equal force in the opposite direction, and the effect of that equal force was to dissolve the Dossman cult.

Polder himself withered like a ringed tree. The bottom fell out of his spirits and powers and imaginations. He believed that he was on Prime World, and that Prime World was the one place from which one might fall into hell everlasting. He would ride his favorite camel out in Longram's Acres for hours. This had been utterly barren land; it had been ceded to a good man named Longram, and it had flourished for him. When it had flourished a bit more, it would be taken away from him, and other utterly barren land would be ceded to him. This is one use to which the influence of good men may be put.

Polder felt that he was at an end, and he had always tried to build many-dimensional lives that could not end abruptly, that could not end at all. The camel, being of primordial and humpbacked flesh, seemed to be Polder's last creature contact. But now even the camel would loft its head, peel back its upper lip, and blink in bloodshot contempt.

And Polder's followers followed him no longer. "I've been given the task of shielding you from adversity," Og Scath said bitterly. "I must hold an umbrella over you, come hell or high water. (My orders were given me in the vernacular, I know not by whom.) I held an umbrella over a boatful bunch in one high water, and I wouldn't want that again. And I'd not like to follow you to hell, but I suppose I must. I've left orders to be called when your death-hour comes, and I'll do what I can for you then and thereafter. But I don't want to see your living face again."

"Do you believe that I might be damned to hell eternal, Og?" Polder asked fearfully. "Do you think it's possible that this is Prime World?"

"Be a little more of a man, Polder," Og said, and his upper lip curled in contempt very nearly like the camel's. "You know that the odds are billions to one against this being Prime World. I mean it though; I don't want to see you alive again."

The mountain-moving effort had finished Polder. And now he came up against the cruelty that is sometimes found in humans, and much more often found in the hybrids of humans and eidolon-men. Most of these fringe folk were of mixed credentials.

"There's nothing more I can do for you, Dossman," Hector Bogus was saying after he had dodged Polder Dossman to no avail. "It was you who broke the Hand of Heaven. It was you who broke all the devices with your mountain-moving caper. I believe I'm relieved of any further responsibility to you. I'll be there to watch at your last destruction, but I don't want to see you again till then."

"Bogus, isn't there some way I could get back to Nine Worlds?" Polder asked with vain hope. "The pleasure goes on there forever, but I am here."

"Polder, have you lost your last wit?" Bogus exploded. "I could ask how you even know there *are* the Nine Worlds, but I will not hide in a fiction so blatant. Polder, you *are* in Nine Worlds. You are there now and forever. You are present nine times in Nine Worlds."

"But I don't know it, I don't experience it, I don't enjoy it. If I don't feel it in this person, then those dimensions of me on Nine Worlds might as well be dimensions of someone else. I want to be conscious of myself being in Nine Worlds."

"It can't be done, Polder." Bogus spoke as if to a malodorous child. "It was your nine persons already enjoying the pleasures there who decided that the pleasures would be spread too thin if less immediate persons of yourself were allowed to share them. Blame nobody for your own greed. Be satisfied with the arrangement. Nine-tenths of you are in the pleasure worlds right now, and the worst that can happen to you is that the other and present tenth of you will fall to hell eternal. You'll still be in good shape on the percentages."

"Bogus, is it possible I will go to hell?" Polder begged for a negative. "Is it possible that this world we are in is Prime World which is one of the gates of hell?"

"I hope it is, Polder. I wish you in hell today."

"You are a coward to be afraid when the odds are so steep in your favor," Moira Mara told Polder when he had tricked her into giving him a minute of her time. "Flip a coin. Flip it twelve billion times. Win every time. If it comes up 'Cities,' then that means this is not Prime World. And if it comes up 'Camels,' that also means this is not Prime World. Or throw dice. Whichever combination of the six sides comes up, they mean that this is not Prime World."

"What if the coin stands on edge?" Polder asked fearfully. "What if a die comes to rest with its seventh side up?"

"Those things also mean that this is not Prime World,"

Moira said. "How can you lose? Try it. It may ease your mind."

Polder flipped a coin into the air, and his fate rode on that flip of the coin. The coin didn't come down 'Cities.' It didn't come down 'Camels,' either. And it didn't come down to stand on its edge. It didn't come down at all. It simply disappeared into the air and was not seen again.

"Hector Bogus, or whatever eidolon-master or Media-master did that, it was cruelly done," Moira railed out of almost her last sympathy for Polder. "He was scared before, and that prank has scared him to death."

Polder Dossman began to cry with his pasty, fat face, the only one of his faces that he had left. Whether some manipulation-master had played a trick with the coin or whether the coin had then come naturally to the end of its existence is not known.

But for Polder, he was on a flopover Jacob's ladder forever, and it took him jerkily down and down. He fell and floundered to the bottom of everything with one clumsiness after another.

Several days later, Polder was declared to be a public nuisance.

Then a writ was obtained for his termination and dismemberment.

And a good man was to be killed by Media machinations at the same time. Otherwise, where would the fun be?

Be he an avid Jump or Jimp,
Be he a crippled or outcast one,
He comes onto (no mind what scrimp)
An end of jumping. This the last one.

"World-Jumper's Ballad"

Polder Dossman lay in the article of death. He was attended by the three outstanding doctors, Vonk, August, and Raphaelson; by their numerous aides; by a coroner; and by a brigadier of police. Their care was not to save Polder's life (there was no chance for that, and no reason for it), but to weigh his death. For this weighing, the men used various equipment.

"Poor old Polder," Og Scath said. Og was filling the office of coroner. "He is not even a main attraction at his own show." For Polder had a "light companion" in death, the good man Longram who had been butchered by the mobs to give some substance of a spectacle.

"His proxy may even have to fulfill some of the basic requirements," said Hector Bogus. Bogus was filling the office of brigadier of police.

"That he shall die with discomfort is part of the requirement," Doctor Vonk said, "but he is beyond any feelings of comfort or discomfort. Longram will have to add Polder's discomforts to his own."

"I have some private ideas of how Polder might be discomforted," Bogus said. "And I'll make them public right at the end."

Longram had been disarmed by the mobs. (That was mob talk for pulling a man's arms out by the roots.) He had been mutilated in a dozen painful ways; and he was still dying in the brightness of his own disposition. But he was given torture gas to breathe, a death potion for himself, a death potion for Polder Dossman. The torture gas will turn the face of the victim into a mask of most hideous agony. Whether that good man Longram remained of bright disposition within is one question; but he was darkly disposed on the outside. Longram's bloody and torturous death had fulfilled the dramatic requirements that Polder was now too empty a person to fulfill. But it was the analysis of Polder that was official and important, so the three doctors bent their efforts toward it.

Doctor Vonk was a man with a huge head, with heavy orbital ridges, with a protruding muzzle on him that made a true chin unnecessary and impossible, with a large backbrain, and with a great good humor. He was a tremendous man with a steep amount of animal in him. And he was an expert at analysis.

Doctor Judah Raphaelson was not so bulky a man, but he was— Wait a minute; he's speaking now.

"Well, was this thing at all alive? Was he of flesh before

someone went to work on him? And of which flesh?" Judah asked.

"Oh, he was alive," Doctor Vonk murmured. "He still is. And he was human, or he had been human somewhere along the way. Human remnants are easily discoverable."

"Well, when was he *made,* then?" Judah asked.

"Oh, not all at once. It was at various points along the way. I believe that several eidolon-masters added to him when it was seen that he was an incurable rogue anyhow. He was an experimental model made by several experimenters."

"You are sure that those are flesh fragments among the eidolon fiber?" Doctor Hans August asked. Hans was a thin and active man. He lifted his head, and his face— Wait a minute; Doctor Vonk has something to add.

"Oh, there're plenty of flesh fragments," Vonk said. "Some of them are human and some of them are regressed flesh. The eidolon and human and regressed are pretty well mixed together."

"The regressed flesh?" Og Scath asked. "Just what is that?"

"Oh, the primordial flesh, what is sometimes called the humpbacked clay (from a passage in Rimskanski, I believe); it's just an idea, a debasement of the old idea of a 'vital fluid'; just a silly idea, except that I have some good samples of that silly idea on the slide now. Ah, eidolon fiber, human flesh, regressive or camel flesh all mixed together. Say, Bogus, how did this man Polder happen to bust so badly?"

"An overload failed. It should have blown quite early in the mountain-moving caper. But the overload failed to blow, and the creature blew instead. Yeah, a thing like that was enough to blow anyone."

"What shall we do about the requirement that this man or movement must have one powerful friend and one powerful enemy present at the end?" Doctor Judah Raphaelson asked.

"Perhaps I can be the one powerful friend," Og Scath said.

"I'm not very friendly to him anymore, but it is written somewhere that I would go to hell for him, or with him."

"Perhaps I can be the one powerful enemy," Hector Bogus said. "Though I'm not very unfriendly to him anymore. It is written somewhere that I will stomp on his fingers as they weaken on his last handhold. I wonder just where it is that all these fateful things are written."

About all that was now left intact and unanalyzed of Polder Dossman was one hand which still held a camel's flem for attribute, and some central masses of the still pumping heart.

"There is a hound and an ariel waiting outside," Hans August said.

"Yes, the brother and sister," Bogus explained. "I suppose there is some fateful thing written about their following him forever. They wouldn't do it without a fateful writing lodged in some murky place. But you, Og, you will not need to follow Polder to hell. You will only follow him down into a shallow and dingy ditch. And that will not be for long: only for a dingy moment."

"He thought this was Prime World," Og said.

"Then for him it was," Bogus told them. "It's a boondocks world; it's a sadly fundamental world. But the odds are billions to one against its being Prime World."

"He thought he'd go from here to perdition or damnation. He said that oblivion was the best deal he could hope for."

"That's the best deal anyone can hope for, Og."

"He was sure he'd fall into hell from here."

"Then, for him, it will be hell, since he dies with his mind set on it. But we'll watch real close. He can't jump again. He has to fall. We'll see where he falls to."

It was about finished. The good man Longram who served as Polder's proxy in some of this was certainly dead. Polder Dossman was dead in ninety-nine percent of him, and what still fluttered would not live long.

"Long enough for a little last fun, though," Hector Bogus said. Hector filled in as a sort of Media and Eidetic Lord on that boondocks world. Hector crudely cut a small sliver of Polder's flickering heart with a pocketknife. Then he pulled several things out of the pockets of his tunic. He gave the heart-sliver a sort of galvanic shock between two little brass balls that were the opposite members of a condenser. "That will keep the flutter going just about long enough," Bogus said.

Bogus put the fluttering sliver of flesh into a small torture cabinet. He bellowed small flames into the cabinet for a white-hot fire.

"It is fun to arrange that even this last flutter-piece of Polder should have exquisite and intense response to and appreciation of pain, and of time," Bogus said. "One can study a soul in hell by this device. That's what I'm doing. In the miniature, so in the fullness. The pain is real to the flutter-piece, and the pain is eternal."

"Did you stick pins into the heads of fluttering moths when you were a boy?" Og Scath asked in contempt.

"No, I didn't," Bogus said. "I didn't begin to do things like that until much later, after other things had failed me. Ah, I'd love to get amplification of its organless screaming! How would you like that, Og?"

"Og Scath is dead," Doctor Vonk said, sadly but with no doubt at all about it. "Quite sudden. He believed he had to go with Polder to shield him. He may have gone an instant early. It still flutters a bit, does it not, Bogus?"

"It flutters less and less, but more and more intensely, in greater and greater agony. I salve myself by saying that this sliver is no more than a toy. I swear that Polder himself was never anything more than a toy. But it's giving a good imitation of a soul screaming in hell, forever. I can't get the amplification to work properly, and now I'm afraid I've lost it."

The Polder-sliver gave one final flutter. Then it stopped fluttering.

"It fails and falls like a spark on the instruments," Doctor Vonk said.

"It falls like lightning," Doctor August said.

"It was his last jump," Doctor Raphaelson said. "When can we record zero? Now! That was it. That was the end of Polder Dossman, forever."

That was the end of Polder Dossman.

For about three seconds.

Then he was heard in the very deep distance, far under the queasy feet of all of them. They didn't need amplification to hear it. And they didn't doubt that all of them would be hearing it forever.

It couldn't, of course, be an actual soul screaming forever in hell. It had to be some sort of imitation.

But it was quite a good imitation.